A Crack in Everything

The chilling sequel to **The River Answered**

By
A.H. Gilbert

Other books by A.H. Gilbert:
The River Answered (An Ash Harrison Mystery)
The Crandall Haunting
For Sissy

For Gibby, who has my heart, always

Prologue

HE was coming.

Ash crouched low in a cedar thicket, bog water pooling around her feet, shivering in the drizzle of the thick, August night. The rain's patter muffled other sounds. Including footsteps.

Was he even aware she was hiding here? He could be miles away. Or he could be squatting in that clump of shrubs, or hovering behind that dead tree, a wavering shadow in the blackness.

Any noise might be deadly. She fought her urge to run.

The water that had soaked her ankles just minutes before now chilled her calves, icy, stinking with earthy rot. She was sinking. Her breath shook as she tried to hold back her panting. The rough tangle of weeds pressed around her.

Every shape shifted in the darkness. Just twenty paces away, a low, jagged shadow seemed to drop into a crouch, so slowly she couldn't tell if she was really seeing it. She stared until her vision blurred and the black shape morphed into a senseless, twitching mass. Her toes and feet burned in the cold water.

A sharp crack cut through the rain, the snap of wood splitting. Fear tightened her stomach, stopping her breath. The sound was behind her, maybe fifty yards back. Too loud for an animal. This swamp held an army of dead trees. Maybe one had toppled in the storm. Or was it him, accidentally snapping a branch? What if he was building something, a fire, possibly a lean-to? Or a trap.

A gust of wind whooshed from the northwest, shielding sounds. She scanned the blackness, seeing nothing but quavering shapes and a glint of movement in the black water.

That noise could be a trick. Maybe he was close, hiding, just as she was, waiting for the moment she had to move.

A low hiss came from the water near her knee, and bubbles rose through the mud. Just a bog sound, probably. But she couldn't help imagining some toothy, clawed, aquatic creature moving beneath the surface, near her feet. Her body jerked in a shudder that ended in clenching shivering. As much as she willed herself to relax, she couldn't stop it. Soon she'd either sink too deep to escape, or she'd freeze to death.

Time to go.

She pulled her legs free of the muck, wincing at the sucking sound. Holding her breath, she rose into a crouch, preparing to run.

Chapter 1

THE sickly sweet stink of rotting human flesh rose stronger than the smoke, stronger than the sharp tang of chemicals.

"Stay here."

Ash glowered at Wyckoff's brusque order, but he didn't care. He didn't need her to see it. No other decomposing animal smelled like this.

He drew his pistol, holding it ready as he passed the smoking ruin. What he sought would not be in there. On the other side, two dark forms lay on the ground.

"Anyone here?" he called. The distinctive "tee-cha, tee-cha" call of an ovenbird rang out, then nothing. The clearing held no other living humans, but he still called one more warning. "Police. Come out. Hands up."

He stood for a moment in the thrumming silence of the deep woods. When the ovenbird called again, he stepped to the bodies, stirring a mist of flies. One of the dead men lay on his stomach, a large bullet entry wound gaping behind his ear. Based on the size of the hole, there wouldn't be much face left. The second man lay on his side. The bullet had entered his eye, blowing out the back of his head. That one still clutched his pistol.

Their remains escalated this investigation into the stratosphere. Murders, a meth explosion…this juggernaut of violence slammed into a town that normally saw little serious crime. And as much as he didn't want to make another mistake that would cause him to miss something, he also couldn't ignore his gut.

His gut told him to keep looking for signs of Graham Novak, both at the cliff edge where Higman was shot and right here in this deadly rubble. That limping, white dog Ash saw there added to his suspicions.

Wyckoff hit the speed dial number for the station.

"Holy crap." Ash stood behind him.

"Get back." He glanced at her to see if she'd stay standing. He'd seen people faint at less. She paled but otherwise seemed okay. "This is a crime scene. Go back behind the cabin. Where I told you."

She scrutinized the bodies before moving away, her hand over her nose and mouth. She'd never forget that smell. No one ever did.

Chapter 2

ROLAND'S text beeped like a bullet into her thoughts. "Time for a call?"

"Sure."

She picked it up on the first ring.

"Hey there."

"Hey gorgeous. Miss you."

She pictured her fiancé's clear gray eyes gazing out through his glasses at their quiet street in Brooklyn Heights. The image elicited … what?

"How are things down there?" She tried to sound cheerful.

"Well, okay, I guess. I found a new game."

"Oh, good. What?"

"It's a strategy game, takes a couple hours. I like it."

If he ever had free time, he spent it gaming. "Sounds perfect for you."

"Yeah, but things would be a lot better with you here. When are you coming back?"

She didn't want to stay alone at Nini's or fight through traffic to get back to Brooklyn Heights. In fact, she didn't know what she wanted to do at all. "I've still got so much to go through here. Nini's stuff. These animals."

"Can I suggest something?" Was that a strained edge in his tone?

"Of course."

"Just hire someone to do it."

The idea stabbed her guts. "How can I let a stranger go through Nini's papers? I haven't even found her will. I'm sure her bank account information is here somewhere. Leave all that to some stranger?"

"No, find a company that does it. A reliable, trustworthy company that dissolves estates every day. Have them box up anything you want to go through yourself and send it home."

Home, a word with a new, uncomfortable hollowness. Where was her home?

"I just can't get myself to do something like that. I'm just… I don't think I'm ready is all."

"When will you be ready?"

Why did he sound like a seventh-grade math teacher?

"When I am."

A silence, long enough to worry her. She always worried he'd learn something that would cause him to want to throw her out.

"I'm sorry. I need to be here a little longer to finish this. It doesn't seem right to leave it to a stranger."

"Is it because Ben Haus is up there?"

His words hit like cold water in the face. Something in her switched.

"The fuck, Roland. How can you say that?" Another silence, heavy with shock. She'd never, ever snapped at him. "Have I ever given you a reason to—"

"Sometimes there are no reasons. Sometimes people just do things." His voice carried an icy edge.

Once the jealousy had been cute, made her secure, relieved that she didn't have to worry about losing him. Now though? She didn't want this conversation.

"Oh, forget it. I have to go."

"What? Wait! Don't go. I'm sorry. It just came out. I'm afraid he'll try to steal you. And you're way up there with a guy you were super-close to not long ago. I start thinking these things when you're not here."

"Yeah."

"Come back here, so I can see your face. So, we can talk, plan the wedding, laugh a little." His voice softened with every word, becoming light. "Like we do. Have fun again. We can't do any of it while you're away."

She sighed. Fun. Such a foreign concept. She'd faked fun for so long, trying so hard to force it to be real. He thought he knew her.

"That's true. I'll get there as soon as I can. I'll take a break from this soon and go down. I'll need to come back up to finish, but at least we can see each other for a bit."

"Oh perfect! Come soon!"

They said goodbye, her heart a tangle. All these conflicting feelings. She needed to talk it through with someone who would always listen and offer insight, albeit sometimes wonky insight that might go in a silly and unexpected direction. She needed Kaitlyn, so she punched the call button.

"Hey, chick! What's up? Ugh, hold on." Ash heard Kaitlyn's panting, then something metallic dropping heavily, a little scream. "I'm at the gym pretending to lift weights. Really, I'm just adding these heavy round thingies to these heavy bar thingies, then I put my hands on it and blow out like a porpoise, then I take them back off and disinfect everything. I'm trying to attract attention, but these guys, Jesus, I swear. The egos!"

Ash chuckled. "It's just possible that they're there to work out and not hook up."

"Ya' think? I think it's a narcissist convention here, with all the mirror gazing they do. All right, I'm leaving. So, what's up?"

"I need your wisdom."

"Oh hell, my wisdom? That's a laugh. Okay, what'cha got? Come on, let's hear it."

"You know about the accident, with Timmy."

"Yeah."

"Well, you didn't know me before that happened, but I used to be different."

"You'll always be different, honey. But we love ya' anyway."

"I mean, I was so … happy. I liked to do things. I mean, I made a living as a whitewater guide. That should tell you a lot. I didn't hesitate to do stuff, wild stuff, a little dangerous. I'd ride horses at top speed and jump bareback over fences. I'd hike on some crazy surfaces. I'd dive into pools of water from cliffs."

"Okay, so you were still different, and you were also crazy."

"Yeah, maybe, but I had so much fun. I loved to laugh and just do whatever."

"So, yes, if you're looking for me to agree, you're right. That's not the person I know. I have to coax you to try new stuff with me, go new places. Sometimes it's like you're kind of afraid or something."

"You're right."

"But now that you bring it up, I can see what you're saying. I could always tell there's another side to you I'm not seeing."

"I'm starting to learn that it's because, after the accident, I kind of shut down. I couldn't even do anything for a long time, and then, when I finally started to realize I had to do something, I found I was afraid to do anything. It's not that I didn't want to. I still am, sometimes. Afraid."

"That's understandable, I guess."

"I haven't been diagnosed by a doctor. But I'm pretty sure I've had PTSD since that accident."

"Post-traumatic Whatzit Disorder? That explains a shitload."

"I think I'm starting to get better. Sliding down that cliff and jumping in after Marco, it started to straighten out the things that have been off-kilter in my head. And then I talked to Ben and realized I'd been blaming myself so hard and that I can stop doing that."

"Okay, that's great, right?"

"It is. I mean, I'm not cured, but I'm heading toward better. And back to my old self, a little."

"Does this mean Ash Harrison is going to be base jumping past my window in a wingsuit or something?"

"Well, I wouldn't go that far, but here's the thing." Ash's pause drew on too long as she tried to find the words, to test them in her head. It was a scary thing to think, let alone say.

"I'm listening. Are you still there or did you walk out of the one tiny cell up there in East Podunk? Do you need to insert another dime?"

"I'm here. I was just thinking. So, when I started my master's a couple years ago, I was pretty messed up."

"And that's when you met me. I'm sure that didn't help your sanity any."

"You were the best part."

"Well, me and Roland, right?"

Ash swallowed hard and took a breath. "I think I chose my degree program based on, on …"

"On what? Something random like the rest of us? Oh! Wait! I'm starting to catch on. Archiving. It's so goddamn safe, right? How can you ever get hurt archiving? Well, you know, maybe a huge shelf in one of those creepy, back rooms at a museum might fall on you."

Ash chuckled, even as this realization left her uneasy. "Yeah, really. Or maybe I'd get my hand stuck in some weird, eighteenth-century monkey trap, and no one would find me for weeks."

"And when they did, they'd just figure you were part of the display, like one of those, what are they called, Wonderamas?"

"Dioramas."

"I can just hear them. 'Wow. We better stick that one in the broom closet. Our visitors would never believe that could happen. Plus, it's so ugly.'"

They both laughed. Count on Kaitlyn to brighten her spirits with random insults.

"But seriously, you're right," Ash said. "I think I picked the safest career I could. I mean, it's in an area that interests me, but the old Ash would rather be the one in the jungle finding cool things, not the one cataloging them."

"Okay, so you spend a hundred grand just to find out you have a useless degree. Join the crowd."

"It's not useless. But I can't even picture myself doing that anymore. I don't even know who that person was, the one who thought that was a good idea."

"Seriously, that happens to a lot of people, but I get it. You're healing, right? And so, you're changing."

"Yeah."

"Well, I just hope you don't want to suddenly dump your college friends, along with your occupation, huh, old buddy?"

"No! Not you!"

"Well, that's a relief. Because I don't know what I'd do without your needling sarcasm to get me through the day. Wait a minute." Kaitlyn's silence stretched longer than usual. "Uh oh."

"'Uh-oh' what?"

"Do you still want to marry Roland?"

Ash stayed silent.

"Ash?"

"Honestly, Kaitlyn, I can't picture that anymore, either. I keep trying to think of going back to Brooklyn Heights and then getting married, and then maybe living like his mother in that huge, hollow mansion in Scarsdale while he's away on business. It's like it's gone, completely unrealistic, because ..."

"Because you're in love with Ben."

"What? No! Well, I don't know."

"Oh, please."

"Wait, leave him out of it."

"As if he's not part of it."

"Well, he is, but even independent of that. Even if Ben and I hadn't talked. I just can't see myself in Roland's world anymore."

"Well, break up with him and marry Ben."

"I don't want to marry Ben. I mean, I don't think I want to get married at all, not right now, but I'm not sure if breaking up with Roland is right, either."

"Well, if you can't see yourself with him, what does that tell you?"

"Maybe that I'm just confused again. Maybe that it's part of my healing process. What if I am in love with him, but I'm so messed up that I don't think I am?"

"Okay, if you keep talking like that, I'm going to be so confused that I'll be the one who needs a psychiatrist."

"What should I do?"

"You want me to tell you what to do? Me? Relationship advice? I haven't had a serious dating prospect for more than a year."

"Yes, I do."

"Okay, here's my advice. Don't go out with anyone. End it with Roland for now. It sounds to me like the last thing you should do right now is get married. And stay out of the sack with Ben. From what you've said, you've had a serious mental illness for several years. You're getting better, which is great. But getting better from PTSD is not that easy, from my understanding, which is minimal, I admit. But you should stop seeing anyone romantically, Ben, Roland, any other boy next door who shows up. You should just focus on getting better."

"I haven't been seeing Ben romantically."

"Well, keep it that way, for now. And even if you choose Roland, you can't go down the aisle as a little broken bird. It's not fair to him, and it's also not fair to switch to Ben under those conditions."

"But what if this is a temporary thing, and Roland is the right person?"

"Ash! Uh-uh. Just no. Stop. Halt. You know that butterfly thing? If you love it, let it go; if it comes back, blah, blah, whatever?"

"Yeah."

"Well. You're the butterfly. It's up to you to decide to fly back or fly away. But don't keep him hanging while you flutter around. Go drink some pollen, jump off a couple cliffs, bungee jump. Whatever it is you need to do. Flap your little wings. That will help you decide what you really want."

She was right.

"Okay, I hear what you're saying. I think you're smart."

"I'm smart? Ha. I talk and whatever comes out, comes out. Anyway, I suggest you get straight to Brooklyn, tell Roland you need a break for a while and grab your things. Is he there or is he on a business trip?"

Roland's job—evaluating and selling potential IPOs—meant extensive travel.

"He's there."

"All right. If you need a place after you talk to him, stay with me for a while."

"Thanks. Hey, smarty pants, I appreciate your listening to me."

"Alright, honey. I'm gonna get a latte with double mocha to replenish all those calories I just burned. Talk to you soon. Love you, weirdo."

Her phone pinged after she clicked off, showing a text from Roland. It had no words, only an image of the two of them, holding hands while riding Pickles and Bumpy toward a sunset. It was a remarkable image because it had never happened. He'd pulled a collection of separate photos and probably AI to create it. She sent him a quick note.

"Wow, you're really getting good at that."

Her stomach flipped as she realized the pain their next live conversation would bring.

Chapter 3

Before

THE setting sun left jagged shadows across Adams when Johnny Jameson chained his bike for his last delivery of the day. He slung his thick, canvas bag easily on his shoulder for the trip to the fifteenth floor. Chicago's famous wind blew cold from the east, and he clutched his coat closed.

"Hi Johnny." Stuart, the doorman, barely looked up from his tablet after buzzing him in.

"Hey." Johnny readjusted his precious bundle against his skinny stomach as he waited for the elevator to arrive.

Once on the fifteenth, he waved to the receptionist through the broad, glass doors of the fancy office. She buzzed him in.

"Hello," he said.

Dark-skinned with bored, brown eyes, she wore her reddish-brown hair short and straight. It might be a wig, because her hair seemed so different every time he saw her.

"Hi." She turned back to her monitor.

He set the envelope on her desk.

"Here you go." He held out his clipboard for her signature. She glanced at the envelope and signed, pressing a button on her desk phone.

"Contract's here."

Johnny wanted to show her, but she might not like it.

She noticed him still there, nodded and said, "Thank you."

"Yeah, sure." She didn't look real friendly, but he just had to share it with somebody. "Hey, you want to see something? Here. Look."

He pulled open his jacket a bit. A little pink nose pushed out, followed by the brown face of a floppy-eared puppy.

"Oh!" Her bored expression dissolved into a smile. "Look at that little guy."

"You can pet him if you want. He's real friendly."

She reached out and received several little licks from the tiny tongue. Johnny liked her delighted giggle.

"Where did you get him?"

"Found him. He was over behind a dumpster near the noodle place on LaSalle. I think somebody might have dumped him."

"Poor little guy. Are you going to keep him?"

Johnny's place didn't allow dogs.

"I hope I can."

A young man in a white button-down and blue tie came down the hall. Johnny had seen him come out before to pick up his deliveries. He quickly covered the puppy and snuggled him down against his belly. These office guys probably wouldn't appreciate a dog in the place. He winked at the receptionist, who smiled back. Well, the puppy had at least seemed to cheer her up.

"Got it?" The man said, looking at the desk through his glasses and reaching for the envelope, ignoring Johnny.

"Yep, last one of the day." Johnny hiked up his shoulder bag.

"You can show him," the receptionist said. "Go ahead."

"Oh, I don't know."

The man looked at him, more impatient than curious. The envelope was more important to him than anything Johnny had.

15

"Go ahead," she said.

He opened his coat to reveal the velvety face.

"A puppy?"

"Yessir. I found it. I think it's abandoned."

"Will you keep it?" The man opened the envelope and didn't pet the dog.

"Well, I don't know. I'm staying at Lincoln Park, and they don't allow pets."

"Lincoln Park?" The receptionist's voice rose. "You mean you stay at the shelter?"

"Yes, ma'am. But it won't be cold much longer, so I might try to hide him until I can stay out."

Both of their expressions changed. The man's gray eyes appraised him with interest, seeming lost in thought. The woman's dark ones were soft. Johnny should be used to this, but shame nagged him.

"It's hard to afford a place in Chicago on a courier's pay. If I find a place I can afford, it's too far out for me to get into the city in time for work. The shelter's not so bad."

"Oh, of course," she said.

"Well, thanks." The man hurried back down the hall with the envelope.

"You take care of that little guy now. Here, let me pet him one more time."

He smiled and handed her the puppy.

"I can't have pets in my place, either." She nestled her nose in his short fur. "I love dogs."

After a moment, Johnny said, "I better take him in case he has to go. That would mess your blouse up all right."

She laughed, handing it back.

When Johnny got outside, he set it down as he unchained his bike. It squatted on the sidewalk, leaving a tiny puddle. Was someone calling him? The voice seemed to come from the alley next to the building. It was almost too narrow for a car, with large dumpsters lining both sides.

"Johnny!" The voice came from the back, where it grew dark.

He stepped in, squinting down the dirty tunnel, trying to focus. Glasses cost too much.

"Hey, Johnny, can you give me a hand with this?"

Now he recognized him. "Oh, sure, okay. What are you doing?" The man struggled with a large wooden pallet.

A few minutes later, Johnny came out. Ignoring the terrified yips of the puppy in the alley, he took off toward the river.

As darkness fell, he pulled up by the scrap yard. It was closed, but no gates blocked its wide entrance. He walked his bike to a metal pile and tossed it on, where it blended with other twisted shapes. A bedframe slipped toward him from the vast heap, and he jumped away. Once back on the street, he kept his head down as he headed toward downtown.

Everything had changed.

Johnny could start anew.

Chapter 4

The Present

NO matter how many times he shuffled his options, getting the hell out of town was the card that always showed up on top.

There was no point in building this stupid fence.

Graham set the last T-post in place and dropped the heavy driver over it. His earmuffs dulled the sharp sound of metal-on-metal as he pounded, the lean muscles on his arms snaking out under his gray tee shirt. Several large rocks guarded the ground, out of sight. They were inevitable, so he usually pounded through. His wrists throbbed from the brutal jarring of metal against stone. He pushed his bangs away from his eyes and checked for Cookie. She sniffed around at the edge of his scrabbly, single acre.

He had nothing here. His job had ripped apart when the Bordens' hardware business collapsed. He winced, remembering Mrs. Borden bulldozing him into dumping the arsenic. Someone would probably find those barrels soon, before they did any more damage. At least he was somewhat employable now, more than two years out of prison and with a solid work history. Not that the Bordens would vouch for him.

"Yes, of course you can get a reference from my past employer. She's in jail upstate for contaminating the community's water, causing fatal illness in several people, including children, and she hates my guts, none of which stops her from blackmailing me. Her husband? I think he liked me okay, but he's dying. Arsenic poisoning. I know. Weird, right?"

That old crocodile might try to use what she had on Graham to cut a deal. But they couldn't charge him if they couldn't find him. One of many reasons to take off.

With the last post in place, he walked to the corner and shoved a roll of chain-link fence from his truck, fixed it to the end post and straightened it along the fence line. The hot, heavy work left him dripping. His stubbly beard itched from sweat. He connected the end of the fence to his truck bumper and slowly stretched it in place. He started clipping it to the T-posts.

Still, he kind of liked it here. In the two years he'd been here, it felt more like home than any other place he'd lived, either with his erratic mother, or in foster care, or, well, jail. Unfortunately, Nini wasn't here.

He prickled with shame, thinking of her, her intelligence, kind words and stale cookies. Ash might stay around for a while, but she didn't know they were related, and she'd never want even a loose relationship with a cousin like him.

If he stayed, Luis would find him. With his two best henchmen murdered in Nini's woods, Luis would focus on Mill Valley. Emo and Bol surely told him they'd found Graham. He would come for him like some debonair Genghis Khan, cracking a whip behind a frothing pack of gun-wielding goons, determined to either murder Graham or enslave him. Because that's what Luis did. He'd get his three-hundred thousand back from Graham, either in cash or blood. But either way, Graham wouldn't get out of this one alive. Not anymore. Not after Emo and Bol. Luis would never forget. Graham could only make it harder for Luis to find him. Leaving town and going far away would reset the clock. In time, he'd pay that debt, when the estate settled. But when? Months?

Years? Anyway, the debt had changed. Money could not be enough anymore. He'd want blood.

"Dear Luis, here's the money you've been pretending I owe you. I threw in extra for blasting open the heads of your little girlfriends, Emo and Bol. Oops! My bad. Who knew their big fat heads were so squishy? Well, guess we're square now, right? Send everybody in the cartel my best. Love and kisses from Hawaii."

Or Tahiti. Viet Nam. Tongo.

He'd get a gig on a cargo ship until the money came through.

He finished the first side, clips in place, fence taut, but not so much that it curled at the bottom. It was good work. He always did good work. That much he could say. He needed more to work with.

Cookie came over, booped his leg with her nose and lay in the shadow of his truck, tongue lolling out in the steamy heat.

"What do you say?" He scratched behind her long, thick ear. "Want to become hard to find? Throw some pepper on the trail?"

Why was Wyckoff still sniffing around, anyway? Higman killed Nini. It should be clear to everybody now. Wyckoff should leave it there. If Graham were half-way across the world, that hound dog wouldn't have a plaything to bat around. The longer Graham stayed, the closer Wyckoff might get to peeling back that last layer.

This worry chewed on Graham, ping-ponging. He was an idiot trying to find an exit in the dark. But his stomach knotted when he remembered his biggest concern.

Someone out there knew almost every detail of Graham's role in the death of two innocent people and the murder of a third. That was reason enough to disappear forever. In a world of flight or fight, flight was the smartest and easiest option. But eliminating this ultimate threat would go a long way in preserving his safety and freedom.

If he wanted to fight, he had to find the caller who started it all. To do it, he had to learn more about Higman. That churlish pig-man. Graham did not regret pulling the trigger.

To find out more about Higman, he needed to find his son. But New York's vast, opaque child protective services had swallowed Marco.

He finished the last clips and surveyed his work. The fence would provide a safe yard, if he opened a business. Stay or go. He must decide.

He'd been a ward of the state during his own childhood. The system protected children with strict confidentiality. There was only one person he could ask.

Graham was not afraid of much. His cool calmness had been one of his greatest assets—so far, anyway. However, he was a little edgy about making this contact. If his newly discovered cousin ever learned what Graham had done to tear her world apart as collateral damage in his ill-planned activity, she'd never want to see or speak to him. Plus, she'd have him arrested.

There would still be time to slink away, disappear like a shadow in the sun. But, in case he was choosing to fight, he had to contact Ash.

Chapter 5

"**WHAT** the hell happened up there?" His chief, Chip, stopped by Wyckoff's desk.

"That's what I'm trying to piece together." Wyckoff and his team had found two more bodies. One was rotting in the woods. The second was hardly a body. The explosion had blasted him to pieces, rendering him into just a few, charred bones. People who cook meth shouldn't play with guns.

He stepped to the community whiteboard, erasing someone else's sketch from an auto accident that had happened weeks ago. Those were the days, when a car crash was exciting. Now, he had murders all over the place. He sketched the key locations.

"Cabin. Woods. Clearing. They were here. He was here with a single Glock. This distance is seventy-four feet, so he was close enough to hit them."

"Yeah, makes sense."

"But that doesn't explain how they were both shot in the back of the head with a shotgun at close range."

Chip raised his eyebrows as he eyed the sketch.

"Do tell."

"That's what I'm trying to figure out. He didn't shoot them, then run to the woods where they then shot him. Those slugs blew their faces off."

"So did the guy in the cabin come out, shoot them and go back inside?"

"That's one possibility. We found a shotgun in there."

"Same gun?"

"Hard to say. It's a mess, badly damaged."

"What are the other possibilities?"

"Another shooter who left the scene."

"Any sign of that?"

"Not really. But how did the two guys in the clearing get up to the cabin? There's only one truck. If they all came together, then one truck makes sense. But if those two guys showed up and surprised the cooks, what happened to their car?"

"Did you find any evidence of them being in the truck?"

"No, and we probably won't. It was damaged in the explosion, and the doors were open. All kinds of debris have blown in. Rain. Squirrels. We'll be lucky to get anything."

"Tire tracks?"

"It's a mud hole. The ruts became channels for water. No tread marks."

"Any IDs on any of them?"

"Yeah, the two guys in the clearing are from Rochester. Nothing on the other two."

"Well, let me know."

Chip walked toward the coffee pot.

That shotgun. The shooter used slugs, not buckshot. And he'd had gone for the heads, not the bodies. Same with Higman. Of course, standing close behind those two guys and shooting their heads was not a challenge, but someone took out Higman from at least forty feet. You could do it with a shotgun, but it was risky with Marco right there. Why not aim for the bigger target, the torso? Any hit on Higman's body would probably have stopped him from killing Marco, if that was the goal. But the shooter had aimed to kill, not disable. And he had both the skills and the balls to take that shot.

Was it the same shooter?

Time to learn more about his corpses. He called his old classmate, Gerry Holmes, an investigator for the state police in Rochester.

"Hey Scott, how ya' doing?"

"Good, good. You?"

"Oh, you know, living the good life. What's going on?"

"You hear about my meth lab fire and the shootout?"

"Yeah, a little bit. Big happenings for your neck of the woods."

"Yeah, well, I think the trouble may have started in yours. The bodies belong to two Rochester residents. Erasmo Ortiz and Bolivar Sanches. Know them?"

"No kidding? Emo and Bol? Oh, boy."

"Who are they?"

"They're Luis Lazcano's key guys." After a pause, Gerry added, "Well, circle the wagons, boys."

"What do you mean?"

"Just be ready. Luis will not be happy about this. Whoever did this is going to pay, and big."

"It's possible they already did. We found the remains of two more guys, one burned in the fire and the other shot in the woods."

"Well, that's probably only the start. Get ready for something more. In case.

"Yeah, well, why don't you do me a favor and nail that guy?"

"Luis? Hah. We haven't been able to pin anything on him, yet. He's never caught holding the bag. He keeps his hands clean, shows up in church with his family. But, between you and me, I think the feds are getting close."

"Good." Graham did five years in prison after he was caught holding one of Luis' bags, literally, a bag of cash exchanged for a bag of meth. "Thanks, Gerry. We'll need to ask Luis what his guys were doing down here, but not yet. I'm still looking at the scene, and I might have more questions for him."

"Yeah, sure. Let me know when you're ready."

So, his suspicion about those two bodies was correct. Were they there to pick up some product? Cash? Or were they there to halt meth operations in the cabin?

Graham lurked in the back of his thoughts. The meth lab was in a cabin hidden deep on Graham's grandmother's land. How did that happen without local knowledge? Graham must be a library of meth operations after his years with Luis.

But the meth lab on one side of the hill was only half his problem. The other half was Higman, whose death on the opposite side was preceded by the sighting of a white dog. White like Cookie.

He'd work it, find the answers. His gut told him that, at the center of this mess, he'd find Graham.

Chapter 6

ASH sorted her grandmother's dishes and cookware into piles: Keep, Donate, Trash. So many things. They cluttered her brain. But it was so difficult to put things in the "donate" and "trash" piles. It was as though the more she handled Nini's things, the more she was stripping herself of her grandmother's importance. She held a fussy, silver, gravy boat. She'd hated polishing it before holiday dinners, but now it felt like the thing was welded to her fingers. Which pile? She didn't want it, but she couldn't bear to get rid of it.

A knock at the porch door made her jump. She expected Ben, but he wouldn't knock on the old, wooden storm door. He'd walk into the kitchen and call "hello."

She peeked out. It took her a moment to realize who he was: The clerk from Bordens' Hardware. Greg? Grant? No. Graham. What the heck was he doing here?

The last time Ash had spoken to this Graham guy, they were bickering like children after she entered the backroom at Bordens' hardware. She'd been chasing a woman she thought might be connected to Nini's death when he stepped in her way. It had caused quite the standoff, made stranger by how familiar he'd looked.

Now she frowned at him through the unlocked door. Why on earth was he here?

"Hi." The half-smile looked out of place on his thin, serious face.

She should lock the door. No. He wasn't threatening, only unexpected.

"Can I help you?"

"Hope so."

She looked behind him at his truck. A white dog with a black patch over its eye sat in the passenger side, gazing at Graham. The window was half down, and the dog had enough space to leap out, but it seemed content. Ash liked dogs that didn't get hysterical in cars. Graham waited, watching Ash's face with a bland, neutral gaze.

Finally, she stepped out, pushing the storm door shut with her foot, still holding the gravy boat. He glanced at it. Were they both assessing how useful it would be as a weapon? No. Not everyone was paranoid.

"Okay. How?"

He stepped back, turning sideways and giving her space. He pulled out a pack of cigarettes. "Mind?"

The smoke wouldn't be that bothersome, outside. She wondered what kind of conversation was coming, with his wanting a cigarette to start it. She shrugged. He lit it as he inhaled, his eyes holding that familiarity again as he looked straight at her for a moment.

"I'm looking for someone you might know." He exhaled smoke as he spoke. "That kid. The one you pulled out of the rapids."

The word caused an instant clench of adrenaline in her gut, and she saw Timmy's hand reaching through green water. Certain triggers still caused her mind to rush back to the day he drowned.

Graham paused, something like concern crossing his eyes. "Marco, I think. Right?"

"Oh, yeah. Marco. You know him?" The local news had rabidly covered the rescue and Higman's murder. Even now, almost two weeks later, reporters tried to find new angles. She saw at least one fresh article a day. She refused to talk to them, but they still bugged her. Wait until they learned about the meth fire and all those corpses.

"Yeah," Graham was saying. "He's a good kid. He used to come by the hardware store. With your grandmother." He looked straight in her eyes again for a second, causing her brain to scan for the old connection she was sure they had. The rich greenish blue in his irises was striking, opaque. He might be handsome if he didn't carry the posture of a pacing cougar on his wiry frame and if he cut that scraggly hair.

"I told him I might have a job for him if I got my business going. It looks like it's going to work out a little faster than I expected, what with the Bordens closing. So, I'm trying to find him."

"Oh!" Finally, a proper reason for this disconcerting man's visit. "Well, I don't really know where he is. Child Protective Services took him. I'm guessing he's in a group home, maybe going into foster care. I'm not sure how that all works or how fast. He probably could be anywhere in the state where they had space."

Graham knew a lot more about it than she did, having stayed in plenty of group homes. Not many people tried to foster him when he was a kid, what with his drug-addict mother always cycling from sober to full-blown user and back again. She'd reclaim him during the dry times and lose him again if she couldn't shake the social workers and truancy officers.

He looked down, took a drag on his cigarette and blew it out, away from her. "So, no idea? No chance he might have been placed with a local family, or any family?"

His interest in Marco still seemed odd, until he added, "I was in CPS sometimes when I was a kid. I think if someone had offered me a job, it might have made a difference."

He gave her that straight-in-the-eye look for a moment, then glanced at his dog and gazed across the street at the barn, smoking and waiting.

"No idea." He seemed legit. "There's someone who might know where he is, though. But I can't give you her contact information without her permission. If you want to give me yours, I can pass it along to her. She might talk to you." It sounded absurdly mysterious, but he didn't respond with surprise or even a joke.

"Yeah, okay. Want me to text it to you?"

Did she want him to have her cell number? She sighed, frustrated again by the suspicions that muddled her. This was part of the PTSD, she'd learned, but it was a reminder that she'd not fully recovered yet. Would she ever again become that happy, trusting Ash? That helped her decide, and she gave Graham her number.

He typed in his phone. Hers, inside, responded with a chime. She stepped inside and checked.

"Okay, got it. I'll let her know you're looking for him."

"Thanks." His shoulders seemed to relax. "It's Graham Novak, by the way." He turned to go, then looked back, nodding toward the gravy boat. "I thought you were going to slug me with that thing."

She held it up, smiling. "I'm trying to figure out what to do with my grandmother's stuff." She started to add, "It's really hard," but why would he care?

"It's fancy."

"Yeah, for gravy, like at a big Thanksgiving dinner. She always used it. She liked things like that. Silver, tablecloths, candlesticks, cloth napkins with rings."

"That's cool. I like it."

On impulse, she said, "Want it?"

"What?"

"Want it? I just can't decide what to do with these things, and there's just so much."

"Nah, it's too valuable. Why don't you sell it?"

"It's not really, just twenty or thirty bucks. It's just … you can take it. Really. If you like it. You don't have to use it for gravy. It can be for anything. I just hate polishing silver. I'd rather find it a home with someone who really likes it."

She held it out. She saw a whirl behind those cloaked eyes.

"Well, yeah. Okay." He took it from her and examined its tarnished pattern. "How do you polish it?"

"With silver polish." She realized he'd been spared that chore his whole life. "You can get it anywhere, in the cleaning aisle. You use a soft cloth that won't scratch it. A dry cloth, a soft brush. Then you rinse off the polish."

He turned it back and forth and lifted it in a quick salute. "Thanks." He started down the steps. "I'll wait to hear from her."

"Okay."

His dog stood as he approached, her long tail swishing slowly.

That long tail and those short legs, the cheerful expression. What was it about this Graham guy? Even his dog seemed familiar. Could it be the same dog she saw on the cliff, the one that distracted Higman?

"Hey, is your dog okay?"

He turned to look at her, still moving toward his car with backward steps. "Yeah. Why?"

"She's not lame?"

He stopped now, his expression hardening, speculative. "No. Why do you ask?"

"Thought I saw her limping before."

"Nope. She's just old and fat."

He climbed in, running his hand over the dog's head before pulling out, giving Ash a wave.

He backed into the road as Ben's car approached. Ben waited before pulling in and parking in the same spot where Graham had.

He strode toward her, grinning. Her heart gave a little rapid patter, as if she were still a fluttery teen. He reached out and grasped her hand affectionately, giving it a squeeze. Six feet tall with intense, light brown eyes and short, dark hair, Ben had maintained a powerful, athletic physique ever since their whitewater days, despite his nine-to-five job as a wind farm engineer.

"What was he doing here? Wasn't that the guy from Bordens'?"

"Yeah. He's looking for Marco. Wants to hire him."

"Small world." Ben looked at the retreating truck as it disappeared around a bend. "Did I tell you it was something he said that made me suspect the Bordens were moving their store to avoid getting caught?"

"What? No! What did he say?"

"I was there one afternoon to talk to the Bordens about our concerns with their new location and, when I left, he was out on the loading dock by the parking lot. He asked if I lived over in the housing development across the creek where all the kids were getting sick. That got me thinking about the Bordens and how they felt they had to move so quickly. That's why I asked Callie if she could find out if there was anything strange in there. Of course, I didn't realize she was going to go all Ninja and break-in during the middle of the night, but, hey. It worked."

Her friend Callie, a former cop and self-defense instructor, had slipped into Bordens', discovering a basement storeroom containing ancient barrels of arsenic before the Bordens tore down their store and hid the poison somewhere. Callie had photographed everything and collected a sample and sent it for analysis. She'd notified a Department of Environmental Conservation agent, who investigated and charged the Bordens.

"No kidding? That's crazy."

"Yeah, weird, right? Now that I think about it, it's almost as though he wanted me to figure it out."

"There's something odd about that guy. I can't put my finger on it. But maybe he did want that. He's … different."

Ash started typing Graham's name into her contacts, but her phone slipped out of her hand. It bounced onto the asphalt driveway and skidded.

"Damn." She picked it up and saw three deep scratches across the back.

"Is it okay?"

"Just scratched, I think." She showed him the damage. "I have to get a new case."

"Yeah. Anyway, I'm still trying to figure out how I know that guy."

———

Ben noticed a rare ray of sunlight glowing across Ash's face and hair as she examined her scratched phone.

"Hey! Look. The sun's trying to come out." She was bright in the golden beam, beautiful. "Here. Got your favorite." He handed her the white, waxy bag and smiled as she peered in, pulling out a plump blueberry scone.

"Yum." She bit into it and rolled her eyes in appreciation as she chewed, glaze flaking onto her shirt.

"Coffees, too."

A light drizzle stole the sunlight, and they climbed the sagging porch steps to sit in the ancient rockers, out of the wet. A happy zing of electricity raced through him. Even the mundane act of sharing pastry with her was exhilarating, after their long, cold separation.

She swallowed and sipped her coffee, a tinge of wariness in her eyes. "Listen. I'm heading back down to Brooklyn tomorrow."

Damn it.

"Okay." It came out cool, and she noticed, one brow raised. She did live there, after all, with that creampuff fiancé.

"I have to take care of some things, but I'm hoping to come back as soon as I can."

"Great! That's…that's great." But what did it mean? "How long do you think you'll be around once you come back?"

She gazed out at the barn. A thin man pedaled by, his clothes filthy, his bare feet black with dirt, his beard growing wild on his face and neck, plastic garbage bags full of who-knows-what hanging off every part of the bike. It seemed like the area's unhoused population was growing.

"I'm not sure." Her mouth set in a thin line. She watched the man pedal out of site, then looked to the heavy, grey sky that now fully blocked the sun.

"What are you thinking about?"

"I've got so much to do."

"Anything I can help with?"

"No. It's not that kind of 'do.' It's things only I can do. And it isn't doing so much as fixing things, well, fixing me." The drizzle became rain, pattering off the roof and downspout.

She seemed pretty perfect to him, except for that irritating fiancé. "You're too hard on yourself. You don't need fixing. Just give yourself room. Mourn your grandmother properly. Take a breath."

Her face hardened before softening into a smile.

"You're right. I'll do all that. But first, I have to go to Brooklyn."

Was she going to break up with Roland, or what? That's all he wanted to hear. But he had enough doubt that he wouldn't ask. It might seem whiny. His frustration pushed him back in the seat. He stretched, running his hands through his hair. "Fine. Well, you don't have to worry about Nini's animals. I'll take care of them." Like he always did.

"Oh, thank you."

He could tell she'd assumed he would. Just the family farm help.

"I could find someone else, if it's too much?"

"I said I do it."

"Okay." Now she leaned forward, looking away, reacting to his annoyance. "I'll see you when I get back then." She stood, holding the paper coffee cup. "Thanks for breakfast."

Oh, so she was dismissing him now? "You're welcome." He stood to leave.

They bordered on glaring at each other. But wait, she was about to walk in the house. It was not how he'd pictured this meet-up. He couldn't let this be their last exchange before she left.

"Hey." He softened his voice.

"What?"

Yes, what? That was the question. What the heck should he say? "It's been great to see you over the past few weeks."

Her cross expression melted away. She snorted a small laugh through her nose and reached for his hand. "It has been great. I…" Her hand was warm and soft, sweaty from the humid air and the coffee cup. "I missed you."

He gripped it, too tight. Hopefully, when she came back from Brooklyn, she would be free of entanglements named Roland.

But Roland wouldn't give up Ash without a fight. Who would?

Chapter 7

MARCO'S call solved the problem of his whereabouts for Graham. Ash's secretive contact had gone directly to the boy, and, atypically for a teen, Marco picked up a phone and called.

"You doing okay?" Graham asked.

"Yeah."

The boy's world was nothing close to "okay." Fleeing his father, hiding with Nini, now both parents dead. The kid must be twisted up with grief and shock.

And Graham caused both parents' deaths, one indirectly, one outright. Plus Nini. Everyone the kid counted on.

"I need your help."

"How?"

"I need to learn more about your father."

"Why?"

"Remember how I found you in Nini's barn and told you where to hide if he came after you?"

"Yeah."

"Did you wonder how I knew him?"

"Yeah."

Graham sighed. He would never tell Marco the truth—or anyone.

"I knew him through a business deal. But now that he's gone, I need to learn more."

"What kind of business?"

"Financial." A safe answer.

"Oh. Well, I don't know anything about his work."

"I need to contact someone he worked with."

"I didn't pay any attention to that."

"Nobody? No names at all?"

"No."

"It's important."

Marco was quiet. Graham waited, smoke clouding around him as he gazed out his window.

"There was one guy. Teresa—that's the lady who told me you wanted to talk to me, the one in the network—she told me her sister is married to a guy who did work with my father. She only mentioned it because she was trying to see if her sister might take me in, so I wouldn't have to be in foster care. Plus, they live in Florida, so I could, you know, go back home, kind of."

"Yeah?"

"But they have a sick kid, so the husband doesn't want to bring in a foster kid. He's pretty young, I think."

An unlikely connection. The woman who helped Marco and his mother escape through an underground network didn't seem like she'd have a brother-in-law who was a soulless crook. But it was a starting point.

"What're their names?"

"I don't know."

"What's Teresa's last name?"

"Um, Lopez."

"Where's the sister live?"

"Someplace on the Gulf."

Not a huge help.

"City?"

"I don't know. Jesus!"

"Sorry."

"Let me think."

Graham waited. He sucked his cigarette and blew out hard.

"Oh! I remember she said they moved to be closer to the children's hospital that could help. Teresa said that her sister was worried because everything was costing a lot, with the new house and the medical bills, and so they couldn't take me."

Teresa probably wouldn't help Graham. Her life, helping people escape abusive relationships, held many secrets. She wouldn't give him information about anyone.

"What's the kid got?" he asked.

"Um, something bad. It was, like, 'batting?'"

Graham turned to his laptop and started a search.

"Is that it? I thought you wanted to talk to me about a job. That's what Teresa said."

"Oh, yeah, maybe. You like dogs?"

"Yeah, I guess."

"Well, I'm starting a dog boarding kennel. I might need help. You in?"

"Yeah, maybe."

"Okay, I'll call you. I got your number now."

He found Batten's Disease and the hospital that specialized in it in Tampa. Was it possible?

He sifted through Higman's social media "friends" and landed on the page of a pretty, young woman named Renata L. Jameson. Unfortunately, her account was private, with no connections identified. But a photo tag showed her in a crowd of people at a booth in an outdoor market. A banner displayed a colorful logo with the letters, "BDSRA."

That turned out to be "Batten Disease Support and Research Association."

Okay, he'd found Teresa Lopez's sister. But where did that get him? It was her husband he wanted. He searched through Higman's other friends for another Jameson but found none. He needed help from someone more sophisticated than he was at this kind of thing. A hacker. But connecting with the one he knew meant reanimating his prison past.

Damn it. He wanted to leave that behind.

But now he had to call Aldrich.

Chapter 8

Before

JOHNNY'S engagement teetered on a pyre of lies. They started with his doctored photo showing a much improved jaw and chin. But that seemed mild compared to the high income he created for himself (lie), the Florida condo (lie), the dead parents who left him a hefty inheritance (lie). The only truth he offered was that his job was stable. It was, but it didn't pay enough to meet his own needs and desires, let alone a new bride's.

Still, it worked to hook her. But to reel her in—get her to the USA—he needed a big influx of cash, for the condo, cars, all that crap. His credit was abominable. But he hadn't always been a Chicago bike courier. In his short, twenty-eight years, he'd lived plenty of lives. His past work with financial cheats had shown him how to skirt the system to get some dough fast, and he still had connections. But he didn't dare risk doing it himself. He had to find a front man.

He met Conrad Higman at a financial services convention in Orlando. The puffy, flaccid-faced bully was as eager to join a get-rich-quick scheme as he was willing to shed his ethics, if he ever had any. It only took a good story, a glittering fantasy and a photo-shopped image of Johnny in an expensive sports car to snag Higman. By the end of the weekend, he'd found that front man and a path to the money he needed.

It was too dangerous to pull this kind of thing often. But he'd soon have enough for a down payment on a condo and a trip to Brazil.

Chapter 9

The Present

WHEN Graham met Aldrich, he didn't realize what a valuable resource he was. He was too busy focusing on staying alive.

When he entered prison at eighteen, Graham's youth and thin stature made him an instant target. But he was deceptively strong and his childhood spent half on the streets taught him to be a fast and decisive fighter, more about survival than style. He hit the vulnerable spots with a fist, elbow, finger, whatever it took to settle things fast and with as little harm to himself as possible. This skill served him well in his first few days in prison, after Robert "Big Slab" Bennett commented, publicly, about the fun he planned to have with Graham.

"Wait until lights out." The brute licked his fat, magenta lips.

Graham sat up all night in the cell corner, clutching a sharpened plastic spoon. Big Slab didn't show that night, but the terrified wait in the dark changed Graham. That was the first, last and only night he was going to spend huddling in fear. He must become the aggressor. After lunch the next day, he saw his opening. He stepped up to Big Slab as they were leaving the cafeteria. Big Slab was five inches taller and at least a hundred pounds heavier than Graham, so Graham had to be fast. He quickly broke the big man's nose with the heel of his hand, then jabbed him in the larynx with his elbow. Big Slab gasped for breath, dropping to his knees and clutching his throat. Graham kicked him in the chin, whipping the man's head back with a shot that probably cracked a vertebra. Graham stayed long enough to make sure Big Slab saw who hit him, then melted away before the guards realized what had happened.

He didn't care if the guards learned he was the culprit. If they ever did, they didn't ask him about it. What mattered is that everyone else knew, and they understood why Graham had done it. Luckily, Big Slab didn't have many friends. The "skinny little guy" gained enough respect to be left alone, and he preferred it that way, avoiding crowds and tight, dark places. He read hundreds of books and took every available class— Barbering, Custodial Maintenance, Furniture Upholstering, Coding— anything to occupy his restless mind and hands as he awaited release.

Aldrich Bell taught coding, the only remote course the prison offered. The first day, the number of students maxed out the class capacity. By the second day, half didn't show up. By the second week, they were down to three. Graham was used to class attrition, but this was extreme. While all the inmates were adept at using smartphones, many of them lack the basic skills to keep up with programming.

But Graham liked it well enough, and Aldrich praised his work.

"Unfortunately, this is the only level they let me teach here," said Aldrich's disembodied voice. Aldrich never turned his camera on. He had a mature, lilting tone that Graham thought of as gay. "They're probably worried one of you smart asses will break into the prison system and open all the gates. But if you get a chance, you should keep going with it. It can make you a good living."

Shortly before Graham's release, Aldrich sent him a note on the prison's lumbering messaging system. He rarely checked it, because almost no one sent him anything.

"Getting out soon? I offer more in-depth classes if you're interested. I'm not just self-promoting. I think you have potential. Look me up."

"Thanks," Graham typed, noticing that Aldrich had sent the message two weeks earlier. "I'll think about it."

Aldrich responded immediately. "Here's my website with the classes I offer. Also, I have much deeper skills than you probably realize. I'm good at finding things, digitally. Just make a note of it. You can't imagine how handy I can be."

"Thanks again," Graham typed. It barely resonated. Was Aldrich hinting he was a hacker? Graham planned to stay out of trouble, so he didn't see a time when he would need one. He also knew people lied about themselves all the time. Aldrich, the faceless voice, seemed a little weird. Why would he make such an offer? At a minimum, Graham wondered if Aldrich might be hitting on him, but he saved his number as one of his few contacts.

He called, leaving his name and number in a voice message. In a couple hours, his phone rang.

"Oh my. A blast from the past. Are you calling to take my classes?"

"No, I remembered you said you're good at finding things, you know, online."

"Ah."

"I could use your help, if you have time."

"Probably."

"I don't have much money right now. But I'll have some soon. I could owe you."

"What do you have besides money?"

If they lived near each other, he could offer handyman help, painting, building, oil changes, plumbing. Furniture upholstering. But Aldrich was some place in the Midwest, he thought.

"What do you need?"

Aldrich was quiet for a moment. "I need someone to play games with."

"Games? What games?"

"Online games. All kinds. Everything from Fortnight to Backgammon."

Graham had played some but found them a waste of time. "Okay, but I'm not very good. How should we do it? An even-hour trade?"

"No, you play three hours for every one I spend putting my stupendous skills to use for you."

"Deal."

Now, would Aldrich deliver?

Aldrich delivered.

His number rang on the burner phone number Graham had shared with him. Graham lived by burner phones. Only a few people had his real phone number—Ash, the Bordens, Wyckoff, his mother, wherever she was. It said a lot about him, what he did and the state of his relationships. It seemed like he spent most of his time avoiding a trace, and the rest of his time preventing people from accessing him.

"Alright, handsome, I have some initial information about this John Jameson you're interested in." Aldrich had started calling Graham "handsome," even though he'd never seen him, at least as far as Graham knew. Then Graham realized that the man might have put his brainpower into discovering more about Graham. It would be easy enough to find his mug shot online. An uncomfortable thought.

"What do you got?"

"Okay, this is just the basic stuff so far. The stuff that's pretty easy for anyone to find. I'm starting a deeper look, but it's getting a little weird, so I thought I'd call you now."

"Let's hear it."

"Okay, I have him born outside of Chicago twenty-nine years ago in a rundown burb called Robbins. He didn't get a high school diploma or a driver's license and ended up as a bicycle delivery driver in Chicago. He used a P.O. Box, so I don't know what his living situation was. Normally, I'd be able to find a physical address, too. But I doubt a delivery driver could afford much of anything there. It wouldn't surprise me if he didn't have a building address. He may have used shelters or stayed with friends or on the street."

"How'd he end up in Florida?"

"Well, if you ever spent a winter in Chicago, you'd know. But, yes, he then shows up in Florida. And here's where it starts to get weird. He rents a posh apartment in Miami Beach and gets married to Renata Lopez. It looks like they have a baby right away. Then he buys a place in Tampa."

"Weird how?"

"Well, here's the thing. He doesn't have a job. He doesn't have any income, at least not on the books. He had to pay a huge down payment on his house and got a terrible interest rate because his credit is so poor. And he's done little to improve it since then. He's drowning in debt, especially for medical things. Between the doctors, the pharmacy and the hospital, he's easily in for half a mill. Not to mention the mortgage and two car payments."

"No job?"

"I have my suspicions that he must be doing something illegal, but I haven't followed that up yet. But no legal work that I've found so far."

Was this the unidentified caller that had told Graham about Nini and the trust fund? This John Jameson sounded like a pretty major loser. If he was the caller, why did he need Higman dead?

"Do you think he somehow made or stole a lot of money before leaving Chicago?"

"Maybe. Maybe that's why he left."

"What else?"

"That's all I got for now."

"It's good. Thanks." Impressive.

"You're welcome. Now, when shall we play?"

Chapter 10

GERRY'S number popped up on Wyckoff's phone.

"Hey, Gerry."

"Hey, how's it going? Listen, I've heard some stuff about Luis Lazcano."

"Yeah?"

"He's on the warpath for someone down your way. Like I figured, he's pissed about his two guys getting shot, and he's blaming it on someone who lives around there."

"Do you have a name?"

"Unfortunately, no. But I would be watching for some of his guys in your area. I think they're planning a hit on this guy, whoever he is. Do you know?"

"I think I do, yeah." Darling Graham.

"Well, you'd be smart keeping an eye on things. Luis doesn't mess around, and this is solid."

"Okay, thanks, Gerry. I will."

Wyckoff hit the "off" button. The head of the Great Lakes cartel planning a hit in sleepy Mill Valley? Mama said there'd be days like this. Damn. He'd been planning a conversation with Graham at some point, but Gerry's warning was urgent.

He drove to Graham's place, surprised to see the new fencing. Now what was he up to? Graham's battered truck was in the driveway. Wyckoff knocked, but the place was empty. He got back in his car and cruised around the neighborhood, guessing that Graham wasn't far. He found him in the cemetery. The tiny graveyard, maintained by the village and a sparse group of prehistoric volunteers from the Daughters of the American Revolution, was one of the few that still had its original iron fencing. Most of them were raided during World War II, the purloined metals melted and used to build ships or other martial necessities. Somehow, this little graveyard off the beaten path had remained unmolested. It made an ideal spot to let a dog run around off-leash. Graham scrolled his phone while sitting on a marble bench near a family stone labeled, "Wilbur."

That dog had a slight limp. Well, well.

Graham glanced up at him, then locked his phone and shoved it in his back pocket.

"What's up, Graham?"

"Not a thing." He pulled a pack of cigarettes from the gray flannel shirt. "Get out of that!" he said to the dog, who had dropped to roll in something that was certainly foul.

The dog came over, wagging her tail in a greeting, a gooey, black smear across her cheek and ear, wafting a decayed stink.

"Hi, pooch." Wyckoff reached out his hand.

"Don't touch my dog."

"Just saying hello." Wyckoff withdrew his hand as the dog sniffed his shoe. He spotted a shaved area on the dog's hip. "Are those stitches?"

"Cookie, go." The dog trotted off happily. "Did you track me here to talk about my dog?"

"As a matter of fact, yes, partly."

Graham squinted and blew cigarette smoke between them. Then he turned to watch the dog.

"There was a white dog up on the cliff the day Higman was shot. A limping dog."

Graham said nothing.

"Did you know there was a game cam hung by that cabin?" True, but the camera had been mostly destroyed in the fire. "We caught a white dog on it." Not true. It was a white blur on the damaged card.

"What cabin?"

"The old cabin on the hill, the one that had been converted to a meth lab. The one that burned to the ground after the meth gasses ignited during a shootout." He paused, considering where to go next. "You know, your old family cabin, up on your grandmother's land."

He'd already observed from past conversations that Graham would be an excellent poker player. When he dropped this bomb, that he knew Graham was Nini's grandson, he noticed alarm flash across Graham's eyes before he regained his calm façade and inhaled on the cigarette. As far as Wyckoff had determined, no one else in the area had discovered Graham's relationship to Nini. Almost no one still alive knew she had a second son, a dangerous sociopath. That son had died in prison, but not before fathering one child with an addict prostitute up in Rochester. Welcome to the world, baby Graham.

Wyckoff had made the connection when he was looking into Nini's death, pushed by the persistent Ash.

"Does Ash know you're cousins?"

Graham said nothing.

"Mind if I look at that injury on your dog? Cookie, right?"

"Yeah, I mind."

"You're going to make me get a warrant to look at your dog?"

"I'm not going to make you do anything."

Both men watched the dog as she moseyed among the headstones.

Finally, Wyckoff said, "Listen, Graham. As you might have noticed, I know a lot about what happened at that cabin."

Graham remained silent.

"You know, even with all the shiny, new semi-automatic handguns those guys used, it was still an old-fashioned, double-barrel twelve-gauge that took out the two cartel guys." Graham wouldn't respond, so he went on. "And it's a funny coincidence that it's the same gun that put a slug through Conrad Higman's head a few hundred yards away and a few minutes later, over on the other side of the cliffs." He couldn't verify that it was the same gun or the timing, but Graham didn't need to know that.

Graham smoked, gazing over the lichen-stained, granite monuments.

"Ash mentioned to me that your grandpa always left a shotgun hidden in the woodshed behind the cabin. That seems like kind of a waste until the day you need it." He let the silence stretch before continuing. "Hey, do you know that I've had seven homicides in the past few weeks? I'm counting your grandmother as the first one, of course, then Marco's mother, Emo and Bol, the two meth cookers. And Higman."

Graham looked at the cigarette in his fingers.

"Do you know how many I have before Higman came to town? Zero. Zero for more than a year. I'm pretty sure it was Higman who shoved your grandmother down the stairs and bashed her head against the floor like everybody thinks, but I'm also pretty sure that whoever put the bullet through Higman's head had reason to silence him, reason to stay in the shadows."

"Cookie, no!" Graham yelled. The dog had gone back to roll and now stood, shook and licked whatever it was she found so irresistible.

"Must be tasty. Anyway, if the shooter had nothing to hide, he'd have immediately identified himself. After all, the shooter probably saved that boy's life. I mean, the first time, from his own father. Ash saved him the second time, of course, from the stream. But I would think that shooter would come forward and describe what he saw. He would have corroborated Ash's description and I, for one, probably wouldn't have charged him. But he didn't do that. Instead, he came out of nowhere and slipped away into nowhere, taking with him a limping, white dog."

Lack of evidence be damned. He was getting close. And if he was right, Graham knew it. He let it all sink in.

"Yeah, I'm guessing that once Higman arrived in town, he was always going to leave Mill Valley dead. It just happened to be convenient up there, on your grandmother's land. Or should I say, your land?" Graham's expression stayed stony. "Isn't that right? It's all yours now, right? Yours and Ash's? Assuming your sweet grandmother would have left something to her son-of-a-bitch of a grandson?"

Graham exhaled sharply and Wyckoff was pleased that he'd finally needled him enough to aggravate him.

"Cookie!" Graham called, standing, his voice annoyed. The dog trotted up, and he clipped the leash on her collar.

"Where you going? I have to tell you something."

Graham ignored him.

"No, I really do. Wait."

Graham turned, his face as impassive as the marble angel on Wilbur's grave.

"You should know that Luis Lazcano is extremely unhappy that his two best guys were killed up there. I've heard he knows who's behind it and is sending some people down here."

Graham's cold eyes shifted to the street for a moment.

"We could keep you safe. I just need to hear the particulars as to what happened up there."

Graham snorted a bit of a laugh, his face showing no humor. "Ask someone who was there."

He and the dog headed out the gate, the dog with that almost imperceptible limp. Wyckoff wondered if he had enough info to get that warrant to examine the dog. He made a mental note to make calls to some vets, to see if any of them had removed a bullet from a white dog's hip recently.

"You know you're trespassing here, right?" he called. "The DAR might want to press charges, especially when they find all the dog crap on their ancestor's graves."

Graham didn't turn around or stop walking, but he held up a full baggy in his right hand.

Damned if the guy didn't clean up after his dog.

Chapter 11

Before

WHEN Johnny's son turned two, things changed. Just a month ago, he'd been walking and kicking balls. Now he struggled to pull himself up. He'd started to form sentences but now was back to mutely pointing.

Every part of having a baby was so expensive, but anything medical was the worst. Debt be damned. He would do anything to make sure his son was okay.

But his son wasn't okay.

After myriad evaluations and tests, expensive and carried out over several weeks, the doctor grimly told them the diagnosis: Batten's Disease.

It meant nothing to Johnny until the doctor said, "There's no easy way to tell you this. Enjoy your time with him. He may make it to eight or nine."

It was as if his own life ended. But Johnny refused to give up. He would find a cure for his son, even if it meant spending millions on experimental medicines and therapies.

Millions he didn't have.

But he knew someone who did.

Chapter 12

The Present

THE DA called Wyckoff.

"Mrs. Borden asked for a plea deal," he said. "She promises to give enough information to arrest the person behind the increased meth use in Mill Valley. In exchange, she wants her charges reduced and considered accidental, not deliberate."

That was a tough one for Wyckoff. The Bordens knew arsenic leached from their store, poisoning the water table and causing the death of two kids in a nearby community, but they hid the crime and the barrels. After hikers stumbled across the barrels, the DEC increased the charges against her since they'd caused further environmental damage. Luckily, they'd been dumped in a flat, level spot, far from water. Investigators found a wadded up "Bordens' Hardware" envelope among the barrels. How convenient.

Wyckoff was certain Mrs. Borden would turn on Graham, linking him to the meth sales.

"I'd offer a deal if and only if her information is good enough to hold up in court," Wyckoff said. "But the arsenic poisoning is not my case. You have to ask Edward Jackson of the DEC. I'll go with what he decides."

Jackson called Wyckoff that afternoon, and they agreed to hear what Mrs. Borden had to say.

Wyckoff didn't know Mrs. Borden well, but her decline was obvious. Where she was once robust and determined, she now seemed excruciatingly thin, sunken and frightened. He noticed a gleam of hope in her eyes when he and Jackson came in and sat across from her.

"You understand that if the information you provide is not sufficient to advance our investigation to the point of arresting a suspect with convictable evidence, that you will not be offered a reduced sentence?" Wyckoff said.

"Yes."

"Let's hear it."

"Graham Novak."

That brought a rush of satisfaction.

"He sold drugs out of my store until I caught him and insisted he stop."

She described how Graham sold the drugs in paint cans to a sleazy kid who drove a Mustang. And that Graham stole a truck from somewhere — possibly the township — to cart away the barrels of arsenic.

When she finished, she'd done a valiant job assigning the blame for all her crimes to Graham. The problem was, she offered little that Wyckoff or Jackson could use in court.

"It's not much, Mrs. Borden, I have to tell you." Wyckoff closed his notebook. "I'll have to see if there is proof of anything you've told us. It'll probably end up a he-said, she-said."

A review of the township's security camera recordings on the date Mrs. Borden identified did indeed show a dark figure taking a truck around midnight, returning it before dawn. The thief—borrower?—

55

dressed in black, including a hoodie, gloves and mask. Impossible to identify. But Wyckoff had enough for another visit to his favorite felon.

Graham wrangled a chain-link gate near his new fence as Wyckoff pulled up. The white dog let out a single, howly bark before getting up and trotting to Wyckoff, her long tail swishing and her face friendly.

"Hello." He touched her head.

"Don't touch my dog." Graham continued working, lean muscles straining over thin leather gloves as he wrangled the heavy frame. "You want to hold this here for a second?"

Wyckoff held the gate while Graham screwed the hinges in place. Once done, he tested it. The gate swung smoothly.

"Okay. What do you want?"

"I want you to come with me to the station. I need to talk to you."

Graham's hooded eyes traced the neat fence line.

"Are you arresting me?"

"No."

"Then, no thanks." He picked up his tools, putting them in a five-gallon bucket.

Wyckoff had expected the rejection. "But I can arrest you, you know. I'm just trying to decide what to charge you with first."

Graham lifted the bucket.

"Let me know when you decide."

Wyckoff smiled behind Graham's back as he walked away, the man's legs looking extra skinny above the bulky, black motorcycle boots. Wyckoff was a good ten years older than Graham, and his own belly already grew firm and round like a bowling ball. It was harder and harder to fight the weight. Graham looked like he'd never gain an ounce of fat on his narrow frame, strong and agile as a leopard. Wyckoff shook his head and followed. Despite Graham's cool rudeness and criminal

56

underpinnings, Wyckoff liked him. He was complicated and interesting and most certainly challenging.

"Shall we talk here, then?"

Graham didn't stop. "Let's say we shan't."

Not too many kids growing up with a junkie mother on the streets of Rochester would pop out with the correct negative for "shall." It sounded like a word Nini would say.

"You are a puzzle, Novak." They stopped at the trailer's front steps.

Graham set the bucket on the landing and reached into his breast pocket for his cigarettes. He put one between his lips and lit it.

"And you're a pain in the ass."

"I'm only a pain in the ass to people who continually appear on my radar in connection with crimes. And you're one of those people."

"Anything else?" Graham put his hand on the front door handle.

"The sooner you talk to me, the sooner I go away."

"Nothing's keeping you from talking."

"You sure we can't find a place to sit down for this?"

"This is fine."

It was awkward, Wyckoff standing at the bottom of the steps, Graham above him. He sighed. "No, this won't work. I'm going to have to arrest you, so we can sit down."

Graham gave him a hard look that lasted probably fifteen seconds. "All right, come in if it's so damned important."

Wyckoff followed him in. It was his first time in the small home, and its lack of personal content was remarkable. There were no photos or artwork and almost no small trinkets that would tell a unique story, just an ashtray and a few paperbacks with second-hand store price stickers. Only one object, sitting on the small, metal-legged, Formica-topped kitchen table, could be called a decoration, albeit a strange one. The silver gravy boat's ornate metal had been crafted in a past century for people very different from Graham. It gleamed in the dusty light, nicely polished. Otherwise, the room was stark and held hints of marijuana under the prevailing smells of dog, soap and cigarettes.

"You have to be careful in these old trailers," Wyckoff said, glancing around for a smoke detector. "You definitely don't want to smoke in bed. They're firetraps. Wooden frames, crappy wiring."

"Are you here to inspect my home or was there something else you want to say?" Graham sat on the couch, so Wyckoff pulled up the only other chair from under the kitchen table. Graham might as well hang a "Visitors Unwelcome" sign.

"Your former employer suddenly wanted to talk to me. She wants a reduced sentence and offered us information in return."

Graham waited, unblinking.

"She told us it was your idea to hide the barrels and that you stole a truck from the town to do it."

Graham sighed out smoke.

"And the township's security camera confirmed it."

"Got a clean I.D., did you?"

"Where were you that night?"

"What night? What time?"

"July 27, around midnight to around 4 a.m."

Graham scrolled through his phone calendar. "A Wednesday. I was here."

"Can you prove it?"

"You can check my phone location, I suppose."

"That just means your phone was here."

"Well, that's enough when you cops are trying to figure out where someone was, right? Don't you use that all the time in placing people near crime scenes?"

"When it's there. Not when it's not there."

"Just when it works in your favor, then."

"Just when I'm looking at someone who's too dumb to leave it home."

Graham said nothing.

"Speaking of dumb, why did you leave the barrels there? Now that seems dumb. You know they had to be found, and fairly quickly."

He didn't expect a response.

"And can you believe we found a clue in there. An envelope addressed to Borden's. What a stroke of luck."

Graham raised his eyebrows.

"I think that your conscience was bothering you. You like the woods and nature. You didn't want to dump poison where it could wreck a stream or poison the ground. You put it where it would be found soon so it could be cleaned up, right? But why did you leave us the envelope, Graham? Are you really that passive aggressive?"

"She's a liar." His tone was flat.

"So, you didn't do it."

"No."

"Okay, then, let's look at the other concern. Mrs. Borden witnessed your selling drugs out of her store, putting them in the trunk of a Mustang, not once, but multiple times. Paint cans? Great choice. It would be hard to find, and the smell would be covered up, at least to human noses."

"She's lying. Did she tell you she tried to blackmail me?"

"Blackmail you for what?"

"Whatever wild-ass shit she decided to make up. I told her to piss off."

"So, you didn't do it."

"Just so you know what kind of person you're getting with her."

"Did you do it?"

"No."

"Pretty creative lie. And did you know, I checked the cabin, and I found the remains of a bunch of paint cans. Isn't that strange? Why would meth cookers have so much paint? Prettying up the place? He had enough to paint the whole forest. I bet when I look through the security footage from Bordens' I'll find you loading his car." He already knew the latter wouldn't pan out, but it was worth mentioning.

"I loaded cars with paint several times a day."

"What was the name of the kid who bought the drugs from you?"

"I don't know what you're talking about."

Enough. He wouldn't get anywhere with Graham, as usual. He stood. "All right then, I guess that's it for now."

He started to the door. The dog was curled up on her fluffy bed by the couch. She didn't lift her head, but her eyes followed him, and her tail thumped. The dog was way friendlier than her owner. White hair coated her bed. It gave him an idea, and a new way to provoke Graham.

"Wow, that dog sheds a lot. I wonder if she left hair up there." He pulled out his notebook and jotted "dog hair" in large letters. "Well, see you soon."

He felt satisfied that this last jab would agitate Graham, if nothing else. Getting under the skin of this guy might help shake loose something. What, he wasn't sure.

Chapter 13

WHEN Ash arrived in Brooklyn, she felt a bubbling dread, hardly an appropriate response to seeing her fiancé after being away for weeks.

The apartment was spotless. Roland always kept things in their place, something she had to force herself to do. For him, cleaning up was automatic, maybe obsessive.

"Are you worried about leaving a trail?" she would joke as he vacuumed and dusted every inch.

She dropped her bag on their bed's smooth comforter, then thought better of it, and set it on the dresser. The extreme neatness of the apartment made it seem even less like home. She'd rehearsed what she needed to say to Roland the entire drive. Even so, her pulse sped up as she imagined it. She could picture a twisted world where she was so averse to hurting his feelings that she just stayed with him. She wouldn't, but it seemed easier than a break-up.

A key clicked in the lock, and her heart thudded. It was time.

Roland's look of surprise at seeing her changed into one of joy.

"You're home!"

He set down his briefcase and hurried to her, pulling her into a long hug, then reaching for her lips in a kiss. Trapped, she tucked her chin as her body hardened. His kiss landed between her eyebrows as she withdrew. He pulled back and looked at her with concern.

"Everything okay?" he asked. He smiled again and hugged her. "I'm so happy you're here. You feel so good. Okay, now tell me, is everything okay? No kiss? Do you have a cold or something? You don't have to go back up there anytime soon, do you?"

"No. Well, yes." His excitement hampered her resolve. "I mean, I have more to do there, but I don't have to go right back, except ..."

"Oh, good. Stay here with me. I've missed you so much." He was touching her gently all over, her hands, her arms, reaching for her, hugging her, squeezing her fingers. "Here, sit. I have something fun planned. I want to tell you. Want a coffee?"

"No. Thanks."

He pulled her by the hand to the sofa.

"Listen, my mom needs help clearing out the cabin. I thought it would be a great chance for us to get away. I'll take a week, and we'll head to the Adirondacks."

"Cabin?" This unexpected proposal distracted her from her goal.

He laughed. "What is going on with you? Are you high?"

She wished she were. She shook her head.

"You know, our cabin, my family's cabin. Up near Lake Colby? Near Saranac Lake?"

She remembered going there for a party after graduation.

"Oh, yeah."

"Okay, so my mom is thinking about selling it. I'm trying to convince her not to. I love it! But she wants to go up there and take a look and at least start cleaning it out, getting it ready in case she puts it on the market. It could be a cool vacation for us. We can drive and make some stops, stay in an Air B&B along the way, do some hikes. Then, once we're up there, we can explore. It's right near the base of White Face."

She walked to the window. The whole idea of this trip was absurd. She and Roland were living different lives with diverging expectations. But it wasn't his fault he thought that she'd love this trip. She hadn't given him any hint that she was planning to end their relationship. The

Ash he knew would have agreed to go on this trip, albeit, with some trepidation, the same as she'd approached anything new for the past few years. It hurt her heart to see how far apart they had become, and how terrible she'd been by not telling him sooner.

"And we can get there well before my mom arrives, so we have it to ourselves for a few days. Then, of course, we'd help with what she wants done, if that's okay."

"Sure." She wanted him to know she wouldn't mind helping, but then she caught herself. "Wait, I mean, no. Hold on."

"What? What's the matter?" He came up behind her, resting his hands gently on her hips, his chin on her shoulder.

"I can't go. Well, I don't think I should go."

"What do you mean, 'should?'"

She turned to face him, backing so his hands dropped off her hips. "I mean, this isn't working for us…for me."

His color drained, leaving his face pale. He realized what was coming, she saw. "What?"

"I mean, I've been doing a lot of thinking while I was alone, and I don't think we should get married."

His expression hardened, his eyes cold. Was this the anger she feared would erupt from the otherwise steady Roland? A concern blipped through her mind. She'd read that sometimes male partners hurt women during break-ups. She shifted subtly, so she was closer to the door before fighting the impulse. That wasn't fair to Roland. He wasn't some brute who got his way by hurting others. Her lingering PTSD was again warping reality.

He moved closer. "Well, honestly, I think we should get married. What's going on? Have you been seeing Ben Haus?" Pain and anger blended in the seething tone in which he said the name.

She'd withheld so much from Roland. He barely knew anything about the accident that killed Timmy, how that caused years of guilt and shame and pushed her away from Ben. He didn't know that saving Marco had jump-started her recovery from the trauma of watching Timmy drown. Had she even told Roland about what had happened up on the cliffs over Nini's farm? No, not much.

She'd omitted so much of herself from their relationship, so much pain. So much history. It made the idea she ever thought that marrying him would be the right thing become, glaringly, the wrong thing. She'd lived the last few years in a dreamland. None of it seemed real, least of all her relationship with Roland.

"Ash? Have you been sleeping with Ben Haus?" He was mad now and probably frightened.

Anger swelled in her, too, at the presumption. But mostly she was hollow and sad. "No. That's not it. I just realized in our time away that I'm not ready to get married."

"When will you be ready?"

"I don't have any plans along those lines."

"What the hell does that mean? We have plans. You and I. We have plans to get married. What happened?"

It was a fair question, yet trying to explain it seemed impossible. Worse, she didn't feel like trying. She sighed, then moved across the open space to the kitchen to make a coffee, just to break free from the tension that encircled them. But he followed closely.

"You need to tell me."

"I can't tell you. It's too long and complicated."

"Who's the new guy then, if not Ben Haus?"

"There is no new guy, but if there were, it would be my business, not yours." Her flaring seemed to surprise him, and it propelled her words. "Our business is us, or what was us. It's over. I'm sorry. I don't think

64

I've been fair to you, ever. I'm not the person you thought I was, and it's not your fault. I never let you see her. Meaning me."

He dropped his anger. She wondered how he did that, change so quickly to calm, his face open and searching, like a skilled actor. "I don't understand, Ash, but I love you, and if there's more to you that you haven't shown yet, I'm here and I want to know that part of you, too. Show me. Tell me. I want to love all of you."

She wanted to cry but wouldn't. So much stayed locked inside. But Roland's eyes were teary.

"Please Ash, give us a chance. Don't do this."

"I'm sorry." She turned away, sipping the coffee, hating this. It hurt to cause him pain. That's what she'd wanted to avoid.

"Please, just come with me to the cabin. We don't have to go as lovers. We can just be friends. My mother is frail. She needs our help, and she loves you so. It would mean everything to her."

She closed her eyes and sighed. She didn't want to be what she felt, which was heartless.

"It would mean so much to me, too. We could use separate rooms. Really. Just come as my friend. We can still have fun that way, you'll see. We always have."

She thought of Roland's gentle, clueless mother who doted on Ash. It probably would be kinder for Ash to break the news to her, or at least to do it along with Roland, to soften the blow. She could say goodbye properly.

Could she handle the trip? Could Roland?

"Well, maybe we can go straight there at the same time she's there, with no side trips and sightseeing."

"Of course! Whatever you want. We can do that. We can chill and enjoy the woods. We can be officially no longer engaged, but just two friends enjoying a road trip."

She heard herself say, "Okay."

"Great, it's a plan. I just need to do a quick overnight to Boston for a meeting. I'm sorry about that. It's an important thing, and I can't cancel last minute. But I'll take the rest of the week off, and we can leave as soon as I get back in the morning."

She sipped her coffee and walked back to the window, looking out over the quiet street, a patch of the gray Hudson distant between the buildings. It wasn't long ago that she could barely look at that river without her heart speeding up and fear creeping through her skin. That unsteady, damaged Ash was fading, but part of her remained, clinging to the idea that the world was dangerous.

Why had she said yes? She could tell he was relieved, but, if possible, she felt worse than ever. Why didn't she just pick up her bag and leave? This trip might only prolong the suffering, Roland's and hers. But it would be the last of him. Of them.

Chapter 14

WAS that SUV slowing down? No. Luis wouldn't send a white SUV. Graham scanned the tree line, then the street.

His paranoia was growing.

His burner rang and showed Aldrich's number.

"Hey."

"Hey. Got something for you."

"Shoot." He lowered himself to the weedy ground, leaning against a post, and lit a cigarette.

"Well, our boyfriend Johnny, he goes to the Tampa airport a lot."

"Where does he fly to?"

"That's a great flippin' question." Aldrich sounded annoyed. "I hacked his car's navigation system. Those things track every place you go, by the way, so be careful."

"I've never driven a car that has one."

"Oh, honey. You must drive old cars." Graham didn't respond, so Aldrich went on. "So, his car goes to the Tampa airport, and we can assume with him in it, since his wife has her own car, and then it sits there for a couple weeks at a time. In a cheap lot, but still, it'll add up."

"Where does he go?"

"Well, that's the thing. It appears that he goes nowhere. There's no record of his getting on a plane."

Graham inhaled the warm smoke. "So, we have a guy deep in debt who has no job but still manages to have a house and two cars, and he goes to the airport and leaves his car for two weeks but doesn't get on a plane?"

"That's what it looks like."

"Makes no sense."

"I agree. But I found something else, something very interesting."

"What?" Cookie, whose eyesight was poor, was looking for him from across the lawn. She trotted toward him with her ears back, listening and sniffing the air, and finally spotted him. She came up, tail swishing, and pressed him in the side with her nose. He scratched her neck, and she collapsed next to him with a groan, panting in the dripping heat.

"Well, I started looking into his phone records, well, you know, his online stuff, the sites he goes to, and I found something really weird. He keeps accessing an account in a New York City financial company. He puts in a user name and password and gets 'read only' access."

Everything froze for a moment.

"Whose account is it?" He dreaded the answer.

"Some very rich lady named Vivian Harrison."

Nini. Graham's mouth grew pasty.

"Read only? So, he doesn't take money from it?"

"No, he seems to go in and look at it. And it has twenty-two million, nearly twenty-three actually, so it's a lot to look at."

"What name does he use?"

"chugeo2. I haven't figured out who he is, yet, but I should be able to soon. Anyway, there are miles more places to search for information about this particular thing and about this John Jameson guy in general, but I thought I'd give you a call because, well, it's so weird."

"All right. Let's see what else you find."

"Now that it's getting so interesting, I'm seriously dying to know why you're after him." When Graham didn't answer, he added quickly, "But I respect your privacy, of course."

68

"Thanks, Aldrich. You do good work. You're actually a little spooky."

"What? Not me."

"Well, something tells me it's better to have you as a friend than an enemy."

Aldrich laughed. "Oh no, I'm harmless. I just poke around."

"Right. Well, talk to you soon."

After he clicked off, Graham sat smoking and scratching the thick hair at Cookie's neck. They had found the right guy, obviously. Someone who knew about Nini's millions had to be the same guy who had contacted Graham. But why was he breaking in regularly to look at her account? Did he look at other people's accounts, too? Aldrich was right. It was strange and unsettling. This guy already knew way too much about Graham, Nini and Higman. Who knows what he might do next?

Chapter 15

GRAHAM needed cash. Had Wyckoff traced Jory to his address at his apartment in town? If he hadn't, Graham might find money there. If he had, the apartment could be under surveillance. The detective never asked him about Jory by name.

It was worth a shot.

He waited until dark, then drove past Jory's modest, second-story apartment. No one seemed to watch it, but he parked on the next block and covered up with a black hoodie and face mask. All these houses probably had doorbell cameras. He crossed through the back neighbor's yard, stopping to scan the area with binoculars, checking windows across the street and cars parked nearby. Except for a few lights in neighboring homes, the street seemed lifeless. Emo and Bol's car sat, trashed, in the rickety garage. Its back door was open, windows down, a cat asleep on the back seat. Its presence was a sure sign that Wyckoff hadn't identified Jory yet.

He climbed the outside stairs to an upper-level porch and slipped on a pair of thin, leather gloves. When he tried the door, it swung inward without resistance, its lock broken. Damn. Some junky had beaten him to it.

He pushed the door wider, looking around the dim kitchen before stepping in. The apartment was cold, AC blasting. He crossed the dining room, carpet silencing his steps, and peeked into the living room. He froze. A man sat on the couch. Or rather, he slumped. In front of him was a pile of meth rocks, a spoon and a syringe. Graham unsnapped the sheath of his five-inch, double-bladed hunting knife.

"Hey."

The man didn't respond. As Graham approached, he saw his unnatural color. He pushed him with his boot, and the guy toppled over onto the floor.

A faint stench of decay rose from him.

The guy must have broken in to find Jory's stash and was so successful that he overdosed. That meth must have made him so hot he turned the air conditioning all the way up before dying. Refrigerated meat.

Graham searched the apartment. He found a wad of cash in the bottom of a potted plant, nearly ten grand. That would help a lot.

He left without taking a second look at the dead man. Let Wyckoff figure that one out, if he ever got his dumb ass over here.

Chapter 16

Before

"MY sister said there is a new family in the network," Renata told Johnny. "A mother and her son."

The network protected abused women who fled from their husbands. The women escaped in secrecy, abandoning everything but what they could carry—or digitally transfer. Whisked through anonymous homes in invisible neighborhoods, they were delivered to a final destination, where they received new identities and a hope to live their lives without fear. It was a hectic, terrifying existence.

Her sister, Teresa, had moved to the US as a mail-order bride ten years before Renata. Her husband turned out to be a brute, and she'd used the network to escape. Now, Teresa worked within the network to help others. She funneled women, often with children, to some of the most remote towns in Upstate New York, where generations of people maintained that stiff, Yankee-farmer policy: Be kind, but mind your own business.

"Her husband is a financial advisor in Palm City," Renata said.

"Really? I know some guys over there. I wonder if I know him."

"I wrote it down." She glanced at a little notebook. "She doesn't usually tell me names, but in this case, she was hoping we might have heard something about him. She's trying to figure out how likely it is he'll come after them. Here it is. Higman. His name is Conrad Higman."

Johnny felt a surge of adrenalin. He'd stopped working with Higman after a few trades. The guy was stupid and a hot head—a bad combination for covert work.

"Doesn't ring a bell."

"Well, if you ever meet him, punch him right in the mouth. See how he likes it."

Johnny nodded, his brain clicking.

"Is she bringing the wife to Mill Valley?"

Mill Valley was Teresa's home, where she worked with several anonymous people to provide safe houses. Sitting west of the Catskills, it was a good first stop for people escaping from abusive partners in New York City.

The little city was important to Johnny for other reasons.

"Yes. They are staying with a family or maybe families—I wasn't sure which—until a final location is found. I think they're going to move farther upstate, eventually."

Johnny was on his way out. Once he was in his car, he called Higman.

"Yeah," Higman sounded angry.

"Hey, how ya' been?"

"I've been better. What's up?" He slurred, drunk as usual.

"Are you missing anyone?"

"What?" Higman's shock and fury vibrated through the phone.

"I might be able to help you find them."

Chapter 17

The Present

"**ALRIGHT,** I think I know who belongs to the username that's used to break into that account," Aldrich told Graham. "I did some digging and found that a man named George Churchman used to work for that financial company. I figured, first three letters of last and first name, 'Chugeo.' That was the way the company set up usernames in the past, it looks like, since I found others like that. He'd stopped working there before he died. What do you think, does that sound possible?"

"Mm, I guess so, but how did this guy in Florida get the email address and password, and why hasn't the company disabled his access if this guy stopped working there?"

"Good questions. I'm not sure I'd want to invest my money there if their I.T. is that lax. On a related note, I'm going to check the passenger lists for flights leaving Tampa on the days that this guy parks at the airport. I might start to see a pattern with someone."

"You can do that?"

"Oh darlin', you'd be surprised."

"I'm impressed. Oh, you might want to check the flights to New York first. This guy called me from a burner with a 212 area code."

"It's possible to fake that."

"Yeah, but it might be worth a look."

Since Borden's was gone, Graham had to go to the big box for fencing supplies. It lay in a strip of commercial chain stores, across from a cheap motel.

When he was walking to his car, he noticed someone familiar leaving one of the curb-side motel rooms. Graham drove on, trying to place him.

Then It hit him. But why was that guy in town?

Graham drove through the Mexican place for a burrito for himself and a chicken taco for Cookie. An anxious memory flicked through his mind as he drove, ending up passing Nini's empty house. With a tightening in his stomach, he pulled over and grabbed his phone, loading up the local newspaper. A quick scan of an old article confirmed his suspicion. Graham pulled back on the road so quickly Cookie lost her balance and looked at him in alarm.

"Sorry, girl."

They were coming at him from all sides. If he wasn't sharp now, someone was going to take him out The odds were against him, and he had to act fast. He was in a killer's crosshairs, and he wasn't the only one.

Chapter 18

THE shooter sat low behind his wheel, a block from Graham's trailer, ducking when headlights glided by in the muggy, starless night. Clouds passed over the half-moon. With his window open, the grinding of crickets and katydids rang loud, along with the occasional gulp of a bullfrog in a nearby pond.

After an hour, an old F150 passed him, the driver looking straight ahead. Graham Novak. Graham pulled into his driveway and lifted his pudgy dog down from the passenger seat before going inside. After thirty minutes, the living room lights turned off and a bedroom light came on. Within a few minutes, that window became dark. The shooter waited another half-hour until, he hoped, Graham was deeply asleep.

He slipped through the back door. It swished on an orange and brown shag carpet, a relic from the 70s. He listened. With a suppressor on his pistol, he could kill the dog without waking Graham, if it came at him. But the house was silent. He slipped across the hall.

The bedroom smelled bad. God, really bad. He stepped close and aimed at the bed, the moon peeping out long enough to dimly light the sleeping body. He shot three times into the center of the torso and waited. Graham didn't move. To be safe, he stepped toward the bed and pulled the sheet down. A car crunched by on the road, its lights illuminating the room. Graham was on his side, facing away, wearing a white muscle shirt and a pair of dark shorts. The shooter fired twice into his head.

He stepped back into the empty street. No one lived close enough to see or hear what happened here. He pointed his car toward the interstate out of Mill Valley. He didn't look back.

It was time to take care of Graham's crazy cousin.

Chapter 19

"**Why** in hell did he open the door?"

Wyckoff scooped up his son as the boy reached for the old cat's tail. Three-year-old Aiden's wail of protest turned into a squeal of joy as his father tossed him high, caught him and pretended to drop him.

"Don't you tease that mean old cat! Oops!"

His wife, Reggie, smiled at the boy's delight as she hunched over her laptop, endlessly prepping for the bar. "When? What?"

"Higman. Why did he open that door?"

"I don't have the first idea of what you're talking about. That killer?"

"Yes." He tossed Aiden one more time, then set him down in front of his fire truck. The boy picked it up and shook it. "I mean, think about it. Let's say he went to Nini's because he thought his son was hiding there. They have a disagreement, and he ends up shoving her so hard she falls."

Reggie's expression hardened. "What a complete and total A-hole he must have been."

"No disputing that. Hey! No!" He grabbed the firetruck before Aiden hurled it at the sliding glass door. The boy let out a wail. "You're in fine form today, Dr. Destructo. Okay, so he's an A-hole with such a bad temper that he would shove a tiny, elderly woman when she wouldn't cooperate with him. I get that. But what I don't get is, why did he open that door?"

"Not following you, detective."

"He didn't just knock her down. He shoved her down the basement stairs, then followed her down and slammed her head against the floor."

"That's enough." She nodded at Aiden, who was watching his father with unnerving concentration.

The microwave beeped, and he pulled out a cup of macaroni and cheese, stirring it, checking its heat and then handing it to the boy. "Have at it."

"You're not going to put him in his booster?"

"Why? Then the booster, the table and the floor will get covered with it. This way, just the floor will get coated." The boy dug in, losing most of the noodles off his spoon before getting one remaining one to his mouth. "To do that, he had to find the basement door. There were, let's see, one, two, three doors in that little alcove. He found the basement door, yanked it open, shoved her down."

He glanced at Aiden, who was busy with his noodles.

"That does seem odd. Did she have it open already?"

"She couldn't physically open it. It had swollen too much over the years."

"Kind of takes the spontaneity out of it, doesn't it?"

"Exactly. It seems less like a fit of temper and more like…Hey, kiddo, that cat doesn't need your food. C'mere, Furrypants." He scooped up the cat, slid open the deck door and plunked it outside where it glared, twitching its tail in irritation.

"Like more of a plan," Reggie said.

"That's what I'm thinking. And if it was a plan, designed to look like a sudden fit of rage, then it seems like he wanted her dead before he even got there."

"Why would he?"

"Well, there you go. That's the question. Why would he want her dead? She probably knew where his son was, so why kill her? And if he didn't want her dead, who did?"

"He's the one who killed her though, right?"

"Almost without a doubt. But that doesn't mean it was his idea."

"You mean someone else could have sent him there, or something like that?"

"That's what I'm wondering."

"Did she have any money?"

"Right. That's the question. Did she have any money, something she might leave to someone? Like a grandchild."

"That girl? What's her name? Ash? You don't possibly think she could have planned it all out?"

"Oh, she could have planned it. But I don't think so. She's the one who brought it all to me. But a grandchild, yes. Another smart grandchild with far fewer scruples."

His wife's laptop screensaver switched on and she wiggled the mouse, refocusing back on the screen. "I've got enough legal puzzles to work through. You have at that, inspector."

"I will." He bent to pick noodles from the floor. "I think it's time to find out what kind of estate she actually had. And just how bad Graham Novak needs money."

———

Staticky voices on the police scanner awoke Wyckoff. A house fire, and it sounded bad. He reached to turn down the volume to go back to sleep when he heard the address, one he knew very well.

Graham's trailer was ablaze.

80

He rolled out of the blankets and slipped from the bedroom. His wife barely stirred. She was used to his late-night calls. He dressed in the extra pants and shirt he kept in the downstairs closet, grabbed his badge and gun and headed out the door.

He got there forty-five minutes from the first fire call, but the home was already a smoldering ruin, flames still blazing in the back. The light rain had been no match for the massive blaze, nor had the fire hoses.

His heart pounded. Was Graham in there?

The Mill Valley fire chief looked surprised to see Wyckoff.

"The police detective?" He was mopping his full, red face with a dirty towel. "What do you know that we don't?"

"Anybody in there?" Wyckoff asked.

"We don't know yet. But I can smell the gasoline."

Wyckoff could, too. The home must have been drenched in it.

It took two hours before they extinguished the fire enough that they could look into the ruins. Wyckoff paced around, his stomach tight. Firefighters in heavy, protective clothing poked through the smoking debris.

"We got one!"

Wyckoff grabbed an extra coat from the firetruck and hurried over. The corpse had little soft tissue remaining. The blaze must have been extremely hot around him for him to be reduced to so little in that short time. His features were gone, and his remaining tissue had shrunk and melted, draped black over the charred bones. Despite the initial impact of the horrific site, Wyckoff could see the exit holes in the skull.

Graham had been shot before the house was lit up.

He sighed, frustrated. He'd had a lot to talk to Graham about. Apparently, someone didn't want those conversations to occur. This meant a long day now, and he pulled out his phone to call for help.

He stopped before hitting the call button as his throat closed, burning. It was hard to believe, but he didn't want that wiseass to be gone. For Pete's sake. What kind of cop mourned a criminal?

"Detective?" A woman came up behind him. She was so small he wondered how she could walk in that heavy, protective clothing and helmet. She caught his stricken expression and paused, evaluating, then handed out a flyer. "Found this in the driveway."

He took it. No, not a flyer, a menu. He held it in his gloved fingers. It was from a takeout curry and bubble tea place in Irondequoit, a suburb of Rochester. Despite being soggy with rain, it was still legible, so not there too long.

"Thanks. Must be a fancy place based on these prices. Good find."

She nodded, then went to help wrangle the fire hose back onto the pumper truck.

"Looks like just the one person in the house," said the fire chief, coming up behind Wyckoff.

"Find a dog?"

"Not yet. Might have found metal from a laptop." The chief walked away.

"Wait. What about a silver gravy dish?"

The guy laughed like he was an idiot. "You mean a blob of metal that could have been a gravy dish?"

"Yeah."

"Nope."

By the time he left, the sun was up, the fire was dead, and Graham's body was on its way to the morgue. He called Gerry, getting his voicemail.

"Hey, Gerry. It's Scott Wyckoff. I think it's time to interview Luis Lazcano. Not only do we have his two, dead bodyguards down here, but I think he just added an assassination to his resume."

82

Chapter 20

LUIS' home was hulking but mundane in the quiet, suburban neighborhood. Set back behind a large, flat front lawn and with an attached, two-car garage, these boxy, Colonial-Cape Cod blends dotted upper-middle American suburbs since the 1950s. This one had upgraded to white vinyl siding. Wyckoff saw the edge of an in-ground pool in the back. A pink and silver kid's bike lay on its side by the front steps. Despite its pleasant appearance, the backyard was just off a busy, four-lane highway, blocked only by a scrappy copse of trees and undergrowth. It seemed like a second-rate location for a cartel boss.

"Really?" Wyckoff said to Gerry, gazing at the house.

"I know, kind of a disappointment, right?" Gerry unbuckled his seat belt. At six-foot-three and about 220, with dark brown skin, short-clipped, graying hair and nearly black eyes, Gerry was exactly the cop Wyckoff liked to be with for stints like this. But it wasn't just his impressive size, it was his cool head and serious, savvy manner that helped in so many situations. They'd interned for the state police together before Wyckoff decided to stay local in his hometown.

"I was expecting a big, fenced estate with multiple buildings and a security gate. Some aggressive Rottweilers loping around."

"Naw, you're out of date. These guys like Presa Canarios."

"What's that? Some kind of bird?"

"Huge fucking mastiffs. Looks like someone beat us to him." Gerry nodded at a couple walking across the yard. They wore shorts and comfy shirts, and the woman held a toddler's hand as the man carried a satchel. They rang the doorbell, and, after waiting a polite amount of time, walked around back.

"JWs?"

"No. They're too casual. I'm thinking some neighborhood thing."

"What? Like maybe trying to enlist him for a Neighborhood Watch?"

"Who better?"

"Do they even know?" This must be the safest neighborhood in the entire city of Rochester, as long as the other criminals realized who lived in the cul-de-sac.

"I doubt it. Ready?"

They got out and followed the couple's example, heading toward the back of the house. An SUV passed them and Gerry nodded at the plainclothes officers in the front seats. It was one of two such cars circling nearby.

His first view of Luis Lascano was as unimpressive as the house. He held a running hose, interrupted while spraying off his pool deck. The couple were now earnestly telling him something, pointing at the flyer as he smiled. Wyckoff saw a kind of imperiousness in his gaze, as if they were children asking for candy. Luis was lean and fit, but not bulky with muscle. He wore a short-sleeved button-down with broad blue and white stripes and white shorts. Rochester must have been seeing more sun than Mill Valley, because his naturally tan skin was ruddy, bronzed and healthy-looking. With his brown eyes, angular face and salt-and-pepper hair, he was handsome and athletic, more like a tennis pro than a drug kingpin.

He spotted Wyckoff and Gerry, and his demeanor immediately changed. He must know them as cops from a mile away.

Luis took the flyer from the man. "Yes, yes. My wife will definitely make something. I'll let her know. She makes the most delicious *cocada*.

84

Do you know it? It's like honey from God. It will sell out. You should price it high." He smiled at his own humor but swept the neighbors away as they thanked him while he eyed the two detectives.

"I take it you're not here about the neighborhood bake sale?" He stepped to the spigot to shut off the hose. He had an accent, and, despite the lightness of his tone, his expression was hard, and when he stepped back to them, there was steel in his eyes.

"What's so important that you interrupt a weekend at my home, with my wife and daughters inside?"

They introduced themselves, and Gerry said, "We need to talk to you about someone you know."

"Who?"

"Graham Novak."

He showed no sign of recognition.

"No, sorry. I don't know that name."

Wyckoff held out Graham's mug shot.

Luis barely glanced at it. "No. Is that all?"

"He sold drugs for you for three years, dipshit," Gerry said. "Your lawyer helped get him a reduced sentence."

"I really don't know what you're talking about."

Gerry showed him another picture he'd found in the files. Taken from a distance, it showed Luis and Graham walking next to each other.

Luis scrutinized it. "May I?" He took the photo, looked at it closely, laughing to himself before saying softly, "Ahh. I always liked that suit. Too bad it got stained." He handed it back. "No, sorry. I don't know him."

"We're trying to find out who shot him and set him and his house on fire," Wyckoff said.

He didn't hide his surprise. "The poor man. Think of it, being roasted like that. Oof." He winced theatrically. "He must have really irritated someone."

"Someone like you?"

"Why would someone like me kill someone like him? It's hard to get anything out of a dead man."

"Like what?" Wyckoff said. "What would you want to get out of him? Did he owe you something?"

Luis chuckled.

It clicked. "Oh! That money the police confiscated when he was caught on the meth drop for you. That was a lot, wasn't it? What, a quarter million?"

"Well, I wouldn't know about anything like that. I'm sure your police files carry details on such petty matters. But it would be very careless, wouldn't it? Handing so much over to the police?"

The realization grabbed Wyckoff like a bear trap. Luis considered Graham responsible for that lost money. "Did you expect to get that back from him somehow?"

"Really, I don't have time for this kind of hypothetical conversation. I'm hosing my patio."

It was arbitrary on Luis' part, but it made complete sense in a thug's world. It was so much money Graham couldn't possibly pay it back legally, not in the timeframe Luis would demand. And if he didn't pay, the consequences would be dire.

"Holy crap." He stared at Luis with a new understanding of the depth of the guy's cruelty.

Luis smiled at him. "I like to do these little household jobs. I find them relaxing, don't you?"

"You were trying to get that money back from Graham, weren't you?"

"Well, again, hypothetically. You know, we're just having a friendly, hypothetical conversation, yes? And if I were trying to get someone to pay me some hypothetical debt, I wouldn't want him dead, would I?"

"If he couldn't pay, you might. If he were intruding in your business without paying you anything, you might. If he killed your best guys, you most definitely would."

"If, if, if." Luis waved his hand as if he were shooing a fly. "It's fun to pretend, isn't it? But generally speaking, people are much more helpful if they are not dead."

"What's your favorite curry?" Gerry asked.

"Excuse me?"

"We found this on his driveway." He showed him the menu in its clear, plastic evidence bag. "Just around the corner from you, right?"

Luis' smile was cold. "I'd guess if you open a drawer in every kitchen in every house on this street you'd find it. Alas, there's not much competition for decent bubble tea up here."

"And it's conveniently located by the highway, so you could stop on your way out of town, before you headed down to Mill Valley, for instance."

Luis shrugged and turned to pick up the hose. "You came a long way to discuss Thai food. And I have other things to do."

Gerry put his big foot on the hose, so when Luis tried to lift it, it pulled out of his hand. He glared at Gerry.

"You know, this is a pretty shabby place they put you, isn't it?" Gerry said. "A big, important guy like you handed this crappy old Colonial in the suburbs? Why didn't they set you up in one of those nice estates down in Victor?"

"We like it here," Luis said, but Wyckoff saw that this was the first comment that seemed to irk him. But he stayed cool. "It's a friendly place for a family. No one bothers you, until you two, of course. If you come back next weekend, you could buy some goodies at the neighborhood bake sale. They're raising money for a new playground."

He wadded up the bake sale flyer and tossed it at Gerry. It bounced off his chest. "But don't come back."

"Do you know a man named Conrad Higman?" Wyckoff held out a photo.

"Never saw him."

"You feeling a little light now that Emo and Bol are gone?" Gerry said.

As if on cue, a beefy man stepped out of the house. He wore a summer jacket that covered all the firearms he probably wore. He asked something in Spanish, scowling at Gerry and Wyckoff, making himself seem bigger and wider.

"Nice of you to show up," Luis said to him. "Did you win your video game?" The big man's eyes darted between Luis and Gerry. "But don't worry about me. These two police officers are leaving now."

"Is this the guy who did it?" Gerry said. "Hey fat boy, you like bubble tea while you barbecue?"

"Hard to find good help." Wyckoff looked the big bodyguard up and down.

The man didn't seem put-off by the insult. He moved closer to Gerry and Wyckoff, putting himself between them and Luis. The hose now freed from Gerry's foot, Luis turned it on and started spraying the patio.

"Good day, officers." Luis turned his back to them.

Gerry nodded at Wyckoff, and they crossed around the house to their car, the bodyguard watching from the backyard.

"That didn't really get us anywhere, did it?" Gerry said as they circled the cul-de-sac and headed out toward the highway. "Just the satisfaction of letting him know that we know."

The couple with the bake sale flyers smiled and waved from the sidewalk, and they waved back.

"The Feds going to be pissed at us?"

"No, they have a-whole-nuther thing going on him. They're close to shutting him down. But they're coming at him from a different direction, through his main guys down in Buffalo. They don't have enough on him yet, maybe never will. These guys put ten layers of other people between themselves and anything real. The Feds might end up pulling the whole thing down but never arresting him."

"Well, I appreciate your help. I did learn something interesting. Graham could never have come up with that money. Not legally, anyway."

"That would make a person pretty jumpy, wouldn't it?"

"Very. If you thought your life depended on it, you might try a lot of things to get enough to pay it back."

"You might."

"A person might even kill to get that money."

"That sounds like a motive to me. You working on something besides this cartel business?"

"I am. And Luis might have helped me solve it."

But his key suspect was now in the morgue, an unrecognizable char of flesh.

Chapter 21

"**WHEN** are you coming back?"

Ben's text brought a rush of guilt. An unspoken expectation stretched between them, almost a promise. Going away with Roland felt like betrayal, of Ben and of her own heart.

Kaitlyn's words rattled around in her conscience. She didn't need lovers; she needed friends. Ben was the best of friends.

"Couple weeks, I think. I promised to help him with a project. But then I'll get back to Mill Valley."

She saw the three dots that meant he was writing a reply, but then nothing.

"Hey, beautiful." Roland came through the apartment door with a cardboard tray of coffee from her favorite neighborhood shop. "I got you something."

"Coffee. Perfect." She reached for the black one.

"And this." He handed her a small box wrapped in tissue paper. She didn't want a gift. Accepting anything from him right now felt like a lie. But he nodded, eyes bright, so she opened it.

"Oh, wow." The rubbery, waterproof, phone case bore an image of Pickles and Bumpy.

She picked up her phone and wiped the dust that had creeped around its edges, noting with annoyance the scratches on the back. She pushed it into the new case.

"It fits perfectly. Thank you."

She liked it but didn't want even this small present from him. She couldn't move on because she'd stupidly said yes to this trip. Now here he was, showing up with a sweet, personal gift.

This would be the end. She'd go with him but finish what she started: Breaking up so she could get back to Mill Valley, settle Nini's business, continue to heal and be friends with Ben. Then she might comfortably allow something more to develop, if it seemed right.

That wasn't exactly as Kaitlyn had advised, though. Why was she identifying herself only in context of being with one man or the other?

Her phone beeped.

"What kind of project?" Ben's text.

"Cleaning his mother's place."

Nothing more from him. She could feel him stewing about this, even though there were 200 miles between them. She sipped her coffee and looked out the window, wanting to tell Ben that she and Roland were staying in separate beds. But really? Did she owe him that or was it still in the "too much information" category of their evolving relationship?

She realized she was wearing her engagement ring. She hadn't worn it much in Mill Valley because it got caught on everything. Roland came up behind her.

"It still looks beautiful on you."

Why had she put it back on? It gave the wrong message. She slid it off.

"I can't wear it any longer." She handed it to him. His face turned pale, then pink with embarrassment. Or anger?

"No, you keep it. Just keep it with you, in case."

"No, you keep it."

He refused to take it. "No! Put it in your pocket. It's yours, no matter what happens with us."

She set it on the kitchen counter.

91

"I told you. I'm not ready for marriage."

"Well, maybe you will be, eventually."

Her throat locked up. She wasn't being forceful enough, and it was because she didn't want to hurt him. It was hard to make him understand without being cruel.

"No, I won't. We're not a couple now, Roland. Don't forget. I'm going with you to help and to see your mother one more time. To tell her myself. I want to say goodbye to her."

"Now come on, don't say that." His eyes were round, brows high. "Let's go and have fun. No pressure. We'll enjoy the road trip and pack up her cabin, help her out, have some laughs. Even if you don't want to get married, we can still have a decent trip, right?"

She saw he was trying not to push too hard. She hated herself for allowing them to come to this place.

"Just so you know, we're going as friends and not fiancés."

"Yes, of course. I can accept that." His tone held forced sincerity. "I'm going to get the car. I'll have it out front in five minutes."

She grabbed her toothbrush and a few other toiletries. When crossing the apartment toward the front door, she noticed the ring was gone.

The worst part of the trip was getting out of Brooklyn, agonizing on a good day, with snarls of traffic and always at least one crawl over a huge bridge. Ash was better about water, crossing water, walking along it, but these long bridges, tangled with cars, still caused her scalp to tighten and sweat and her heart to flutter.

She scrolled through her phone when they crossed the George Washington, pretending they were not on a nearly 5000-foot bridge, 200 feet above the dark, fast Hudson. A text from Kaitlyn popped up.

"You're around this week, right? Let's have lunch."

"Next week, yes. Going to help Roland's mom this week."

"Oh! That's weird. Well, have fun."

"Long story."

"Who are you texting?" Roland's tone was snappish.

"Kaitlyn."

He glanced at her phone, which made a low-battery buzz.

"I'll tell you later," she wrote. "Phone's dying."

As Kaitlyn's "thumbs-up" came through, Ash fumbled around for the right cord and plugged it into the car jack, propped in the console. Ignoring Roland's suspicion, she shut her eyes. A nap would get her out of city traffic and away from the river.

She awoke when Roland picked up 87 in Harriman. From here, the route was pretty and scenic, miles of small towns, and random, single homes interspersed with long stretches of flat farmland. As they got closer to Albany, the route became hillier, woodier, then suburban and finally, metropolitan as the capital sprawled before them. Its striking architecture was a blend of an old, port city combined with newer, still-growing businesses and government buildings.

About thirty minutes later, Roland signaled to exit. They were heading toward Saratoga.

"Where are we going?"

"I have a surprise for you."

"What kind of a surprise?"

"The surprise kind." He smiled. She didn't return it, so he added, "It wouldn't be a surprise if I told you."

"Well, I don't really like to be surprised." A waspish edge crept into her tone.

"Well, we'll need lunch, even if you don't like the surprise, so just relax and trust me."

She sighed, annoyed. He pulled into downtown with its lovely, old, columned buildings, specialty shops and restaurants, stopping in front of a cute business labeled, "Springs Spa."

"I know you've been tense, so for our lunch break, I booked you a spa treatment."

"You what?"

"A facial, Swedish massage and full use of the pool and sauna for three hours."

"Three hours?" What kind of nonsense was this?

"Yes. I want you to just enjoy it. We need a break from the road. You deserve to be treated to something really special. I want this to feel good, to help you relax."

She imagined telling him what she thought: "I don't want some stranger's hands all over me." But that would hurt his feelings. He was trying to do something nice for her.

But still.

"I don't really need something like this to relax. I mean, it's not going to help, and I don't think it's a great idea to tie up three hours of our day when we're supposed to be in Colby Lake tonight."

"It's just a break. We'll still get there. Don't reject my special treat." He was pleading, hurt and hopeful.

She sighed. Why did he do this? Why was he so prone to doing things he thought were right, using no imagination or truly taking the time to see who she was? Ash was not a spa person. Probably, in his mind, women were supposed to like these things. But Ash didn't. He didn't ask. He assumed. Was he trying to be some generous, gallant knight to…to what? Impress her? Show her what a great husband he'd be?

She wanted to get away from him for a while, and the spa was as good an excuse as any.

"All right."

"You don't have to sound so miserable about it." She'd wounded him, and he showed it without hesitation. He got out and walked around the car, opening the door for her. It felt more like an expulsion than a courteous gesture.

"Sorry." She climbed out. "Uh, thanks. What are you going to do?"

"I'm going to play nine holes at the state park course."

Ash didn't play golf, but she still would have traded places with him. She'd much rather be outside, swinging a club around after a little ball than lying on her back while some strange woman prodded her blackheads.

"All right. See you in a few hours." He tried to kiss her forehead, but she pulled back. He ignored it and went back to the driver's side. "Really. You'll like it. Just go with it."

She waved with a weak smile and turned to the spa. It was in a huge, three-story building probably built when Saratoga was first becoming a rich tourists' destination, back in the 1800s. It filled half a block and housed multiple merchants, with its two-story gray columns and enormous picture windows overlooking downtown. She was familiar with this quaint area long known for its healthy mineral springs, performing arts and gorgeous horse racing track. Maybe she'd duck out and head over to the park, but Roland still stood at the driver's side of the car, watching, grinning his encouragement. So, she walked up the steps between the pillars and entered the aromatic mellow of the spa.

Chapter 22

"TAKE off the dress," Johnny's hands gripped Christi's waist, his whisper coarse in her ear.

"Really?" She grinned but scanned the area for others.

"Really."

The overlook was empty. He'd taken several photos of her, and some selfies with her in the background, her skin glowing in the cool light of the mid-afternoon sun. It gave her pearly dress an almost blue glow. Across the narrow valley, the mountains stood dark. He could barely hear the roar of the river, some 300 feet below.

"So, you're finally ready?" She leaned back into him, pressing her tight bottom against his groin. "I was beginning to wonder. Okay, then. Can you get the buttons?"

He undid the white, cloth-covered buttons at the back, and she wiggled out of the dress and its stiff petticoat. She was standing now in a one-piece camisole and bra, both virginal white.

Hah, that was a laugh.

Though it was August, it was cool here in the mountains, and her nipples showed clearly through the thin fabric in the chill. At any other time, the sight would arouse him.

"Want another picture?" Her tone was coquettish, irritating. She didn't get it.

"Not until it's all off."

"Oh?" She smiled at him, her eyes lustful and naughty. She peeled off the remaining pieces. "How's this?"

She should win an Oscar for this performance.

"Gaze out at the scenery." He lifted the camera.

She turned. He flipped the camera strap over her head and against her throat, tightening it.

"Thanks for everything," he said. "You'll never know what it means to me."

She fought. But there's only so much fighting a small woman can do when a thin strap is cutting through her windpipe. When she dropped, he kept it tight. What was taking so long? His arms ached and his back cramped while she struggled, pulling at his hands, weaker and weaker. When she stopped, he counted to sixty before loosening it and checking her pulse. Nothing. He'd let her lie for a few minutes, just to be sure.

He stuffed the dress and underwear in the car and strolled to the overlook. Swift clouds cast rippling shadows across the trees and valley.

When he checked her again, no life simmered in that beautiful body.

He dragged her to the farthest edge of the overlook, the steepest, away from the entrance. His back protesting, he pulled her up on the rock wall and shoved her over. The distant rustle of the river hid the thud of her corpse hitting the rocks below. He looked down. That might be an arm, still visible.

Eh, he wasn't worried. This was a remote, unmarked and rarely used overlook. Anyone who stopped would walk to the center of the wall, where the view was most impressive. It was unlikely anyone would see her before she was only bones.

And if someone did notice her, who cared? She was just one more dead whore.

Chapter 23

ASH waited in the lobby for Roland, pummeled, prodded and poked. Her annoyance with this surprise spa idea outweighed the benefits. She'd flatly refused to entrust her pores to the attendant who wielded an array of menacing-looking, surgical steel tools, but she'd allowed her face to be smeared with various, spicy-smelling creams, followed by a tight mask, and accepted the deep back massage and hot rocks.

She watched her phone. Her text thanked Ben for taking care of Nini's animals while she was gone, but he'd not seen it yet. She tried calling Kaitlyn to fill her in on where she was going and why, but it went right to voicemail.

"Hey, it's me. I told Roland I'd help him and his mom, but it's the last trip I'll be taking with him. I let him know I'm ready to end it. He's not really accepting it. But I thought the least I could do was to help him, and especially, for his mom …" The voice mail beeped, cutting her short, and she clicked off.

Her inability to connect with her two favorite people left her lonely. She tried to scroll through social media, but the cell connection inside the old building with its thick walls was poor, so she gave up and thumbed through a magazine.

Twenty minutes later, Roland's text told her he was out front.

"How was it?" he asked, grinning. He smelled clean and soapy. He must have showered in the golf course clubhouse.

"Great." She glanced at him as she fastened her safety belt. "How was the golf?"

"41."

"That's good, right?"

"Yeah, I'd like to come back and do all eighteen sometime. It's a fun course." He pulled out onto Broadway and headed north. "I figured you wouldn't want to stop, so I picked up some sandwiches for the road. In the back."

She grabbed the bag and rummaged through, finding an onion bagel with hummus and muenster. Credit to Roland for getting her favorite.

"Which do you want?"

"I'll take the roast beef."

They ate in silence. He seemed to have a buzzy energy, but she was sleepy after lazing around in the heat of the spa, especially with her belly now full. She fell asleep, slumped against the door.

The car jerked violently, waking her as it lurched over uneven ground. They were in a thick forest on a rough, tar-and-chip road. Dusk darkened the woods.

"What's wrong?"

"Engine's cutting out."

"Where are we?"

"I took a shortcut over the mountain." Roland sounded confident but perhaps masked a hint of worry. The car seemed to act normally now, but the road was rough.

"What? Why?" In the six-million-acre Adirondack Park, shortcuts were not likely to be short, although they would be cut—as in, cut out of the side of a heavily forested mountain. Pines, firs and birches enclosed this narrow road, so dense as to almost be claustrophobic, with no glimpse of a view through the thick trees and undergrowth.

"We still had such a long way to go, and I knew you were tired. Anyway, I've been this way before."

She still heard his doubt. "Really?"

"Yeah, sure. I think so. It's been a while." He had to slow the car as the surface became gravel and the potholes worse. There was no way to turn around here if they wanted to. The road was far too narrow.

She checked her phone but saw no new messages. Nothing from Ben. He must be upset. She texted, "I should be back there before the end of the month." A red bar across the top of her phone showed she'd lost coverage.

The car jerked again. "Why is it doing that? How far are we from the cabin?"

"About thirty-five miles, last time we had a connection."

She tried to determine where the sun would set. The trees were too thick. "What direction are we traveling? Is there anything nearby?"

"This road crosses southeast to northwest. I believe."

The car jumped again, jolting forward, pausing, then jerking ahead again.

"What's going on?" Ash tried not to panic, but her anxiety was increasing. She fought it back, never sure anymore if it was a symptom or if it was really time to worry.

"I'm not sure. It could be the fuel filter." He stopped, shifted to Park and got out. She couldn't sit still so hopped out to see what he was looking at when he opened the hood.

He wiggled some lines. "This all looks okay."

She'd never known him to study car engines before, but she hadn't, either.

He got back in and started the car. It purred to life, then jerked.

"Damn it." He got out and slid underneath the engine.

She looked around at the darkening woods. "What the hell? Where's the nearest town, or garage, or home, or anything?"

He climbed in and turned the key. The car sounded okay, so she climbed in. But they only got a few feet before it surged and then stopped. The dashboard dinged a warning.

He looked at her uneasily. "It's going to be okay. We just have to make a plan."

"A plan? The plan was 86 to Saranac Lake, then 3 to Trudeau. That was the plan. This! This is just ..."

"I'm so sorry. I thought this would be faster. I was trying to get you to a comfy bed for the night."

"Yeah, well, how'd that work out?" This stupid detour. Stupid trip. Why did she say yes to it all? She sighed, trying to squelch the rage. Obviously, he hadn't intended to have car problems. That wasn't his fault.

"Well, we can either stay in the car for the night or we can try to find a phone—or a cell—to get some help." He held his phone's flashlight over a paper map.

"It's not real smart to start hiking now. It's almost dusk. I think. It's hard to tell in here."

"Yeah, but if I'm reading this right, we're very close to a hamlet. Look. This is where we turned on the shortcut, this road. About five minutes ago, we passed this fork. See that?"

"Yeah."

"So, if this is correct, there's a hamlet right there. I think if we go about a hundred yards west, here, we'll see the lights over that way."

"Maybe." It made sense, but since she'd been asleep, she was disoriented.

"I think we should walk to here. That will be this break in the trees. If we get to this spot and see this meadow, we'll know we're really close to that little crossroads. From there, we can decide if we should keep going."

Ash did not want to spend a night sleeping in this car, only to be no better off in the morning. But neither did she want to get lost. The region near Roland's family cabin was notorious for people going missing. All directions carried a risk of disappearing forever.

"I think we should try it. Just go that way." He pointed at the woods, left of the road. "And go straight about one-hundred yards. Then we'll know. If we're still in woods, we turn around and come straight back. If we're at the valley, we go across and get to a house."

The woods already looked much darker than the thin slash of road. Ash was not afraid of the woods or any animals within them. But traipsing through these particular woods at dusk bordered on fool-hearty, which she also was not.

Or was it her PTSD trying to take control, giving her an extra dose of anxiety about doing something, anything, out of her usual routine? It sometimes still could wrest control of her nervous system. Was this one of those times?

"I'm going to give it a shot," he said. "I'm going to walk that way. I'll count to two-hundred steps. If the valley is there, I'll come back, and we can go together. If not, I'll come back, and we'll spend the night in the car and decide what to do in the morning."

"Do you think splitting up is a good idea?"

"Three minutes there; three minutes back. It's not even splitting up, we'll be so close."

Was he trying to prove something? The fragile ego behind this idea was probably aching from her announcement of a break-up. Maybe he thought if he saved them from this, he would be a hero, the man she wanted to marry again. He was wrong. Even if he were successful in finding help, there was no way she would ever be the Ash he thought she was three months ago. They could never go back.

"If you feel you must do it, then do it," she said. "But you need to be back in ten minutes, or …" The word hung there. Or what? What would she do? She doubted either of them knew.

He was suddenly close to her. Was he trying to kiss her goodbye? She twisted her head and received his kiss on her temple.

"Be safe." She tried to soften the fact that she'd widened the already open wound. She so regretted this prolonged break-up.

He draped his knapsack over his shoulder and crossed from the light of the road into the shadows of the woods. Within a few strides, he disappeared. She checked the time on her phone and waited. Until now, she hadn't noticed the constant, metallic chirp of the crickets near her feet and in the undergrowth, their vibrato providing background music to all other evening sounds. The trees grew darker as the last light slipped away.

Then a scream pierced the darkness, freezing her brain and heart.

Chapter 24

BEN'S throat was so dry he couldn't swallow as he read the text again.

"Being back in Brooklyn made me realize I want to be with Roland only. We're getting married this weekend. Sorry to tell you by text." It was punctuated by a "sad" emoji.

"What the hell?" He checked that it really had come from Ash, then read it again. Tossing the phone on his couch, he stepped to the picture window overlooking a fallow field, his eyes focused outward, but his mind churning.

He pressed the call button. If she was truly breaking up with him—not that they were far enough in their relationship for that—he would hear it from her mouth, not from some text with a stupid emoji. That's why the text seemed to come from nowhere. They weren't lovers. And you don't send a text like that to end a friendship.

"This is Ash. Please leave me a message." Her recording.

"What the hell, Ash? You just sent this text. I know you're near your phone. Pick up!"

He clicked off and called again with the same result.

"Damn it."

He typed in the text box. "WTH? Call me."

He'd agreed to guide an overnight fly-fishing trip with a couple from Jersey and was due to pick them up soon. He'd like to get out of it, but they were waiting.

Was he also in denial, refusing to accept the message's validity? The text seemed so off. Ash admittedly had an odd side—which he usually found charming—but this didn't even sound like her. A sad emoji? Really? On such a harsh note? No call? Just a text, precipitated by nothing? Had he been so wrong in thinking that he and Ash were finally on the path to romance?

No. He wasn't wrong. And she wouldn't pull something like this.

He clicked Kaitlyn's number. She never had her phone far and always answered calls.

"Hey, Studly. How's my shoulda-been husband?"

After he and Kaitlyn had gone out a few times when she was visiting Ash in Mill Valley, she realized it was a farce before he'd even admitted to himself that he loved Ash.

"Hey, how you doing?"

"I was so excited to see your call I spilled my toenail polish, and now I'm trying to clean it up, so I don't lose my goddamned apartment deposit. That's how I'm doing."

"Hey, have you heard from Ash recently?"

"Yeah, and it was kind of weird. Why?"

"How so?"

"She said she was going to be gone all week, helping Roland's mom with something."

"When did she send that?"

"Let me check. What's up, anyway, Inspector Clouseau? You're digging around for something."

"She just sent me a text saying she wants to be with Roland and they're eloping, so, sorry, sad emoji."

"What? No way. Damn it! Now I have it all over my elbow."

"No way what?"

"She told me she was breaking up with him when she came back. That's what was so weird about the texts. She said she'd fill me in later, but later, she left me a quick voice message. I've called but haven't heard back from her. Yesterday afternoon, 1:03 p.m."

"Breaking up with him?" Despite the terminal communication from Ash, his heart thudded.

"Well, yeah, duh. What the hell is the matter with you two? You're like, who is that couple who could never admit they love each other? Rhett and Scarlet? Yeah, you're like them, the anti-couple couple."

"Where was she going?"

"She said she was helping his mother. She's in Scarsdale, I think. Something about cleaning out a house. Would that take a week?"

"Yeah, she said earlier she was going to clean, but why a week?"

"She couldn't have lunch with me until next week. Scarsdale is only an hour away."

"I don't know.'"

He heard her scrubbing as he pondered this. She must have him on speaker.

"So, she ended it with you by text?" Kaitlyn said. "Ash is usually a lot classier than that. And by the way, are you even at a point where it can be officially ended? I mean, have you two even slept together yet? I would think I might hear about that earth-shaking event. Or at least feel the shaking."

"Where else might she need to go to help his mother? Any other homes that you know of?"

"Wait, let me think." He listened to the scrubbing. "And by the way, I noticed you ignored my question."

"Mm-hmm."

"Okay, okay. Let me think. I think … Yes! I think that was…That graduation party in the woods."

"What? Where?"

"I couldn't go because I had a big date with a chubby schmuck with bad breath who later became a brain surgeon. I really think I might have been able to tolerate the breath if I'd known."

"Where in the woods?"

"Up in the Adirondacks somewhere. I think his family had a cabin up on a lake."

"Where? What lake?"

"Seriously? Do you know how many lakes there are in the Adirondacks? And even more big ponds that people call lakes? I don't remember. Only that it would have been about two and a half hours to get there from Albany, so I couldn't make everything work, you know, juggling that and the stinky, would-be brain surgeon. You know, when I went out with him, he was studying yeast infections or warts or something."

"Can you remember anything else about it?"

"Not right now, but I'll let you know if I do."

"Okay, thanks. I might be hard to reach because I'll be camping tonight, so if I don't respond right away, that's why. But let me know."

"Okay. You know, when we get married, that camping bullshit will have to stop."

He had to smile. "Okay, sure. Talk to you later. And thanks."

Chapter 25

THE scream sounded half-human, half-animal and so close. There it was again. Oh, okay. She knew that sound, the warning cry of a fox. It was probably responding to Roland's presence near its burrow, trying to either scare or lure him away.

In the distance, she thought she heard the soft, deep hooting of an owl.

Her phone told her the ten minutes were up. Roland should come back through the woods. She listened, but the constant insect buzz drowned other sounds. Now eleven minutes after eight, the sun had officially set, but it still cast a dull gray light on the road. She wouldn't have long before darkness completely enveloped the hill, so she had to go quickly, if she was going.

"Roland?" She didn't want to venture into the forest, but he might need help. Even if he were safe, she couldn't bear the idea of being alone in the car, waiting in the dark with no phone service and only her own agonizing thoughts. She climbed out of the car. The rich, damp scent of the leaf-covered ground mingled with the clean tang of the pines.

She thought she heard another sound, a call. She held her breath and listened. Yes. Was it an animal? No.

"Help!"

"Roland?" She moved to the edge of the woods, a border she hesitated to cross.

"Help! Ash!"

She had to try. Turning on her phone's flashlight, she took a deep breath and crossed into the darkness. A few strides ahead and behind, the trees were silhouettes. Only those shapes in her immediate reach had color in the gray twilight.

"Roland?"

No answer. Was this the right direction? It was too easy to get confused and just walk in circles. Sometimes searchers found bodies of lost hikers within short distances of their last known location, with evidence showing they had walked in a circle, hopelessly lost, until they died.

"Hello?" She stood still, listening. Was that an answer? She walked on.

The light brightened ahead as her feet caught on branches and rocks. She stepped out of the trees and took one more step. Oh crap. She was on the rocky edge of a cliff, the woods, and the mountain, towering above. She gasped. It was so close. Far below, a broad, flat area could be the valley that Roland thought he saw on the map. But no. There was no hamlet across there, no house lights. There was nothing down there except more wilderness. Wherever this was, it was not the spot Roland had identified on the map. Ash's stomach bubbled like it was full of beetles. But what she saw next made adrenalin blast through her muscles.

Roland's backpack hung on a shrubby, striped maple at the cliff's edge.

She stepped forward, leaning away from the edge, reaching for it and yanking it back. That spot, at the cliff edge, showed disturbed ground, possibly by something heavy—someone?—sliding there. Vertigo rocked her as the darkness below seemed to move. She dropped to her knees and leaned over, bracing on her hands.

"Roland!" she yelled into the blackness.

Far away in the darkness, the fox's scream was the only answer.

Ash sat back, bewildered. Was Roland gone? Had he really fallen over the cliff?

"Roland!" She waited. Her voice echoed through the night. Not even the fox or owl called back.

She swept her phone flashlight around her. The battery might die before she got back to the car, but could she see anything that might tell her where Roland had gone? The light fell on the backpack. Why had he taken that from the car? She stood, not sure what to do.

A big, bright beam appeared, hurting her eyes, completely engulfing her. Confused, she used her hand to block it. She heard three, pounding footsteps and tried to duck. A powerful blow jerked her forward.

As she fell, Ash's shoulder slammed against a protrusion in the cliff, flipping her in the air. She scrabbled at the cliff wall, her fingers and nails tearing raw on the sharp rocks. In the pitch black, the fall seemed endless. Branches of a cliff-edge shrub scraped her skin. She grabbed it. The thin branches cracked and ripped away, but she slowed. She slammed flat on her back and smacked her head.

She opened her eyes, blinking in the darkness, now seeing stars, brilliant but blurry, at the cliff's edge above. Had she passed out? Everything hurt. Her vision slowly cleared. She reached out with one hand, finding the edge of the thin, rocky ledge. Her head pounded. The pain in her shoulder made it hard to breathe. She tried to sit up, and the shoulder shifted with a resounding pop, bringing instant relief. Ugh. It must have been dislocated. She found sticky wetness along her leg and side. The wounds burned under her touch.

The bright light glared from above. She had no place to hide, so she froze as it passed over her. Who did that? Was it some maniac who killed Roland and shoved her over the cliff?

The light went out.

Her stomach twisted with nausea as she sat up. Her thoughts seemed scattered. Leaning against the rock wall, she passed out.

A sharp reverberation woke her. Little stones seemed to leap at her face as a throbbing, percussive ricochet sounded. Gun shots? She tried to regain focus, searching for the shooter. The spotlight again. A bullet hit near her feet, rocks pelting her. She dragged herself up, flattening against the cliff side. It was at least fifty feet to the top and thirty to the bottom. Below lay an open field, but the steep mountain cliff bottomed out in huge, sharp boulders as big as cars. Another shot. No time to think.

She slid to the edge, then lowered herself over. Losing her grip, she fell a few feet, grabbing a shrub and balancing, one foot on a rocky bump. The moon hung huge and orange between swift clouds. She saw another foothold.

Sliding along the shrub, she let it bend under her weight as she reached her toe for the protrusion. She stopped on another narrow ledge and vomited over the side. A rumble rolled across the valley. A car? Jet? No. Thunder. The wind rattled the nearby shrubs. The rain started as a few slow, large drops, quickening. Thunder boomed, echoing around the valley as lightning flashed. This rain might cause that spotlight to reflect on the drops, shielding her from view. If he was even there. She'd lost track of time.

She noticed a fissure running down the wall, wider toward the bottom. It was her best chance. She stuck a foot in the crack and, clutching small irregularities in the rock, eased down. Her fingers, already injured from her initial fall, burned and bled. Near the bottom, she lost her grip and fell, landing on a basketball-sized boulder. A sharp snap in her side came with brutal pain. Now, every gasping breath was excruciating. But she was at the bottom.

Is this how he kills me? Bit by bit until I'm too damaged to keep going?

As the rain sliced her with icy droplets, and the lightning flashed all around the isolated landscape, she clutched her rib and ran into the field. The soft, meadow ground seemed to help her feet spring as she chose a path into the middle. But no. The ground wasn't only soft, it was moving. It bounced under her, rolling like a waterbed. A bog!

She realized it too late as the sphagnum mat folded under her weight. She plunged into the icy water, tangled with moss and sour strings of slime. The mat sprung back like a trap door. She no longer saw the lightning or felt the razors of rain.

Chapter 26

"**LOOK** at Ash's IG but be ready."

Ben had dropped the fly-fishing couple at their hotel when Kaitlyn's text arrived.

"Now what?"

He opened the social media and scrolled to Ash's page. A picture showed Roland and Ash, heads pressed together, displaying wedding rings on their fingers and grinning.

"It's official," was the only comment, along with "#newlyweds," and "#honeymoon." Other pictures showed Ash entering a spa for a "pre-wedding splurge." Another, captioned "Honeymoon hideaway," showed her standing on a rocky overlook, most of her face turned away from the camera.

His face burned as his brain sizzled.

How could she do this to us?

No, this was wrong. Nothing about it made any sense.

Had Ash transformed into a Stepford Wife? The tone of these posts didn't match Ash's style. Nor did the concept that she would elope with someone whom, a moment before, she planned to leave.

He studied the photo of Roland and Ash smiling and showing their wedding bands. The picture had been edited, he thought, so the hands were prominent, and Ash and Roland seemed blurred.

In the spa photo, she looked back with a serious, doubting gaze. It wasn't the expression of a bride-to-be, heading for some pre-wedding pampering. The spa building looked familiar, and he put it through an image search.

Okay. Downtown Saratoga.

So, Kaitlyn's memory of the approximate direction of Roland's family camp was right. The Adirondacks stretched huge to the north of Saratoga. But, as Kaitlyn had pointed out, a family cabin could perch on any one of thousands of other lakes and ponds in the park.

He hated the pictures of her and Roland on the overlook. Only a bit of her profile showed, while Roland leaned in to kiss her. It was another edited photo, making her hair seem a little blonder and her chin less defined. Why were these pictures so heavily doctored?

Ben's personal despair and flickering hope might mislead him, but he was certain that there was a lie here. If he was correct, what was really going on, and where was Ash?

The photo showing them holding out their rings was familiar. What's more, Ash's lower arm was bare. He recognized the shirt she wore and was pretty sure it was long-sleeved. Why would the sleeves be edited out?

Time to dig.

He searched Ash's online photos, all the way back to her grad school shots, but he found nothing like the engagement photo. He tried to do the same with Roland, but he was almost invisible online, and tight privacy restrictions guarded his rare social media accounts.

But Kaitlyn's were wide open. There, he hit gold. He found the same picture of Roland and Ash, smiling together, but they weren't showing off their hands. They were each holding part of a turkey wishbone. The next shot showed them pulling it apart. Yes, Ash's shirt had long sleeves.

Ben reexamined the wedding ring photo. Now that he knew the source photo, he spotted the careful editing of some other couples' hands into it. What was going on here? Why did they want to create this elaborate hoax? The confusion gave way to anxiety, even fear. Maybe only one of them manufactured this lie.

Was Ash in trouble? He had to find her.

He searched through Kaitlyn's hundreds of photos, going backward in time through her grad school experience. There! Kaitlyn was tagged in a photo of people on a rustic deck of a classic, Adirondack log house— hardly a cabin, more of an estate.

"Where are you, Kaitlyn!? We miss you." The location: Lake Colby.

He checked online maps and found it near White Face Mountain.

At last! He'd found the place to start his search.

Chapter 27

BLACK water. Cold.

A tangle of submerged weeds grabbed her like fingers. Ash thrashed as they tightened around her, her lungs already demanding air.

From the blackness, Timmy's white, wrinkled body bobbed, so close she felt his cold skin. She almost screamed out what little air she held. She would die in these weeds. Not of drowning. Of fear.

No, Ash. It's not real. Calm down or die but think fast. She saw Callie's down-turned smile, heard her saying, "Just slow your roll, kid. Relax. You've got this."

She forced stillness into her mind and body. Callie said to know the terror is there, but don't let it take over. Just acknowledge it and refocus.

You can swim. You are strong. Water is not scary. It's water.

She had only seconds. She looked up, searching for a hint of daylight. A glimmer flickered, so far away. She couldn't swim through that tangled rope wall. She fought panic as she tried to decide.

Against all instincts, she pushed downward, deeper into the blackness. At the bottom, the roots and weeds were sparse. She pushed along, fingers squishing into the rocky mud. Something squirmed under them. After crawling for thirty feet, she was desperate. She looked up and sprung, her hands together and pointing like a missile toward that spot of light. She got a few feet before the tangle stopped her, its tendrils wrapping around her and holding her down. Her lungs burned, bursting.

Her heart thudded, urging her to breathe. But inhaling water meant a horrible death.

She clawed and climbed and tore at the roots, the glimpse of sunlight coming closer. Finally, her hand pushed through, ripping at the softball-sized hole as she shoved her nose and mouth through. She gulped the fresh, cool air. Her heart slowed.

She half-paddled, half-pushed against the weeds, but couldn't get enough leverage to make the hole bigger. Okay, she'd pick a direction and go from air hole to air hole, scrambling along the bottom like a crayfish. Hopefully, the water at the bottom would get deeper. If it got shallower, she would have no way to get out. She took a huge breath and scuttled to the bottom, looking up. She saw sunlight about forty feet away and crept along, then clawed up for air.

Timmy's body bumped against her, waxy in the weeds.

No. That's not real. Keep going.

The sphagnum grew thinner, and the layer of water at the bottom deeper. And was it actually...flowing? Follow the flow.

The next time she popped up at an air hole, she got her whole head through. She could see open water. It must be the deepest part of the bog, where weeds hadn't grown—the last open water remaining from the original lake. She'd head toward it. She looked around as she inhaled one more deep breath, preparing to dive.

What was that?

Her head was already under the weeds when it registered. A man! He stood some twenty feet away, looking straight at her. She pushed back up into the air, turning as far as she could each way, searching. He was gone.

"Hello?" Her voice was weak and hoarse. "Hello? Help! Are you there?"

Crickets. Literally, crickets, all around her. She was about to yell again, but a tingle of fear surged from her stomach, closing her throat, halting her call. It could be the shooter.

But she chilled as the realization hit. He looked like Roland.

He'd stood quietly, watching her struggle, so close, not moving, not helping, studying her like she was a tile in one of his strategic, board games.

Was this another hallucination? But it seemed so real. No, he would have helped her. It must be another trick of her mind, like Timmy.

But she'd never hallucinated Roland before.

The urge to flee hit like a knife in her spine, and she took another huge breath, ducking into the acidy darkness. This time she could swim freely under the sphagnum. She must be getting close to the lake. Through the weeds, she saw light opening above her and she pushed up, emerging in the black water of the lake. She floated on her back as her head throbbed and her rib ached. This was barely better since she couldn't cross the thin sphagnum at the lake edge without falling in again. She was stuck here. She searched, unable to see past the weeds along the water.

Her concussed brain whirred. She needed to breathe, float, relax.

Had she really seen someone? No, he couldn't have been real.

She held her breath, straining to hear through the pound of her heart. She sensed he was out there, waiting.

Chapter 28

WHAT a joke to call such a luxurious residence a cabin. Roland's family must be wealthy. At least the wiener had that going for him.

Through the window, he saw sheets covered the furniture, and across in the kitchen, the refrigerator door stood open.

When he met Roland after Nini's funeral, Ben was unimpressed with the measly nerd. No one else was good enough for Ash, but Roland carried an icky artificiality — a kind word for the creepiness Ben sensed.

Kaitlyn's disclosure that Ash planned to break up with Roland nagged at him. Was he capable of hurting her? Hard to believe the determined, smart and once confident Ash picked someone who might be violent with her. But she'd become so vulnerable since Timmy, she might overlook traits that she normally would eschew.

Nobody had been in this cabin for months. But he had no other idea where to search.

Maybe she really had gotten married. No, he knew in every cell that she had posted none of those gross social media pictures or gushed on about eloping, just as he was certain that she hadn't broken up with him by text. It was wrong. He must find her.

He drove south, stopping at the scant restaurants and convenience stores along the way to see if anyone recognized her. No luck.

Forty miles south of Lake Colby, Ben sat in his car outside a dirty little gas station whose employee was kind enough to share a Wi-Fi password. With almost no cell service along the route, Ben crawled with anxiety, worried he might miss a note from Ash or Kaitlyn and not able to see if Ash—or someone—made any updates to her social media. Turned out, there was nothing new but a note from Kaitlyn telling him she had no updates.

As he frowned at his phone, a text came through from a number he didn't recognize. It contained a link that he would normally never open, assuming it was spam. But the note along with the link made him read it twice.

"This is Ash's last location. Get there fast."

The link took him to a photo of an interactive map with a pin showing satellite coordinates. This was not the typical Google map. Most people couldn't track an individual so precisely. Was it from a cop, like that detective in Mill Valley or perhaps Callie? Could he trust it?

"Who are you?" he typed.

The quick response: "Trust it."

"How do you know? Who are you?"

He received nothing more. Who the heck sent it? What if this was a cruel hoax? But what if it was accurate? It was better than nothing.

He punched the coordinates into his phone's map. The location sat in the middle of nowhere, no towns or roads nearby. He had to zoom out before he found anything that was named—the Raquette River. Not much help. He bought a paper map from the gas station, in case he lost the satellite connection.

"You know where this is?" He stuck his phone in the gas station attendant's face. The guy wore a brown, plaid flannel shirt, dark green, canvas pants, a home haircut and a scruffy beard. He looked at it for a while, using his fingers to zoom out and back in.

After a moment, he said, "Oh, yeah. You know where that is?"

"No." Obviously.

"That's by the bog at Gacy Mountain. I been there."

"Where is it? What town is it near?"

"Um, none. It's nowhere. Let me think. Okay, maybe punch in Axton Landing. That might get you sort of close."

Ben tried it. The landing was ten miles from that pin on the map.

"No road?"

"No, that's all hiking. It's dangerous, too. You can sink into the bog, and then it's lights out. There's a rough road that goes up the mountain, here." The clerk unfolded the paper map and drew a circle. "That's the bog. This is the landing. This…" He drew an arrow. "Is a road. It would take you a long, back way toward the landing. It's right by the bog, but you couldn't get into it very well from there, as I recall. It's a tall cliff."

Ash might be there.

"Got bottled water?"

He bought a case and headed toward the cliff. As he tried to stay on the curving roads at high speed, a nagging worry pricked his consciousness. What if the anonymous person giving him the location tip wasn't on his side? What if someone had kidnapped or otherwise hurt Ash? That same person might send Ben in the wrong direction, into a dangerous bog, luring him into a trap.

Chapter 29

BEN almost missed the car tucked behind a hedge of shrubs and scrubby saplings. He approached, holding his breath. Yes, it was the same model that Ash drove in Mill Valley. Inside, it was neat, no telltale wallet, hat or clothing that would hint at the former occupants. Leaves gathered on its hood, stuck by dew and rain. Bird droppings on the roof were both fresh and old. An orb spider's delicate web hovered between the side mirror and the window. He tried the doors. All locked.

Oh well.

He grabbed his hatchet and smashed the driver's side window with one, hard blow, then unlocked the doors and slid behind the wheel. The inside contained no personal items, not even a car registration. As he groped around for the trunk release, he noticed the driver had been short. The trunk held two suitcases. His skin tightened when he found a soft, extra-large man's T-shirt with "Mill Valley Grind" on the front. But a man didn't wear that shirt. He was with Ash when she bought it at the coffee shop to wear as a nightshirt. She'd said she normally slept in nothing, but with Kaitlyn staying with her, she didn't want to scandalize her should they collide in the hall at night.

He'd found Ash's car. But where was she?

He tried 9-1-1. No luck.

He knew something about tracking. But the stakes were high. He had to pick the right way. He spotted a slight disruption in the leaves leading into the woods and followed. Probably a deer trail. When he got to the cliff, he stood high above the sphagnum bog. That clerk had given him accurate information.

He cupped his hands around his mouth. "Ash!"

The only response was the choppy siren of a downy woodpecker.

"Ash!"

Nothing.

He had to get to that bog. He walked back to his car and grabbed his camping gear, stuffing as much bottled water as he could in the backpack. After a moment of consideration, he added his water purifier. The five protein bars he found in a box behind the driver's seat would have to do, along with some electrolyte gummies.

It had been years since he made a rappelling harness out of a rope. It would be horrendously uncomfortable, but he'd get to the bottom, probably alive. He attached a pulley on his line and secured it to a sturdy white pine. After adjusting the leg loops so he'd still have all his parts when he reached the bottom, he lowered himself over the edge.

He went way too fast, his hands and arms burning as he used his feet to bump down the cliff. It was much harder to hold his own weight than he remembered. He landed hard on the rocky bottom, nearly turning an ankle before dropping backward, hitting his tailbone on a rock. After catching his breath and flexing his stiff hands, he yanked the rope down behind him and stepped out of the harness. He didn't need to examine his skin to know he had abrasions on his thighs from the rope.

"Ash!"

A raven, overhead, offered a raspy "*haw*."

Seeing what might be a trail, he started out, treading carefully on the buoyant surface where the scratchy, wild cranberries and pitcher plants stretched far into the distance

Nearly an hour had passed when a series of beeps and buzzes came from his phone. He must have crossed into a short cell zone. He ignored

123

most of the messages—from Kaitlyn, potential camping customers, a coworker—and focused on the second message from the anonymous texter.

"Her latest location."

The link took forever to load. Finally, it showed a dot in the bog. He zoomed out and tried to glean where it was in relation to him, his heart thudding way too hard. Was he being guided by a friend or not? He sighed and shut his eyes. He heard the rain before he felt it, pattering on the bog plants' thick leaves. Tipping his head back, eyes still shut, he let the light sprinkles touch his cheeks.

What was he supposed to do? He had to decide. He was out of time.

Chapter 30

THAT bright area had to be a pond. He tested the footing. Too dicey. He climbed the dry, white trunk of a fallen tree. What was that shape? He squinted through his binoculars.

"Yes!"

Ash lay along a thin log that jutted from the lake, clinging like a spider monkey. His heart pattered relief.

"Hey! Ash!" There was no way she could hang on like that unless she was conscious. "Ash!"

He wanted to jump in and swim to her, but the moss mat around the pond was too thin. He'd fall through before he could get to the lake's edge. "Ash!"

She shifted her head.

"Ash!"

Her face turned toward him. He waved both arms as she lifted her head, turning his way, then slipped into the water. It looked deliberate, but what if it was because of exhaustion?

He thought he saw her face hiding behind the trunk. "Ash! It's me! Ben! It's Ben!"

"Ben?" She pulled back onto the trunk. "Ben?"

"Yes! It's me! I can't get close."

"I know. I'm trapped."

He pulled out his rope and secured it to the tree, then tied a thick stick to the other end and tossed it into the center of the pond. High weeds blocked his view of her.

"Ok," she called.

He pulled. Getting her across the pond was easy, but it was another matter when she hit the thin mat.

"Try lying flat and hang onto the rope. Distribute your weight and crawl on your belly. I'll pull."

He strained like a draft horse. The moss collapsed under her weight, but between her scrambling and his yanking, she finally reached firmer ground. She came on hands and knees, her arms sometimes dropping through the mat. At last, she reached him and sat wordlessly, eyes wide with an unfocused, frightened gaze. He dropped to the ground and pulled her into a hug.

"Ow!"

"What?"

"Rib."

He relaxed his grasp.

"How did you find me?"

"You won't believe it." He grinned. "I can't believe it."

But his smile faded as he noted her condition. She was raw on almost every portion of exposed skin, her clothing torn. She shivered, and her eyes seemed dull and exhausted. If he hadn't found her, she'd be dead from exposure in hours.

"Come on," he said. "Let's get the tent up and start a fire. Here."

He handed her a bottle of water. She drank, pausing once to gasp before gulping it dry. She barely chewed the electrolyte gummies before swallowing them down, then lay back, hand on her stomach. Her eyes seemed to follow something overhead. When he looked up, he saw a bird, high up. A strange bird. No. A drone?

126

She tried to rise, grunting in pain, clutching his hand for support.

"You're going to have to tell me what the hell is going on. But first, we need to get you warmed up." He pulled out a reflective, plastic sheet and wrapped her, glancing up. The bird, or drone, was gone. "It's a thermal blanket. You'll feel warmer soon. Let me look at you. Yeah, your pupils are different sizes. How'd you knock your head?"

"I went unconscious."

"Hmm. Let's go slowly." He started toward the shadow of the woods circling the huge wetland. "We'll go until we find the first decent place to pitch the tent. I'll get a fire going, warm you up. Then you can rest."

"No. Someone is chasing me."

"Who? Are you sure?" He searched the bog. It showed no signs of life, not even a bird. "Who?"

"I don't know. But we have to go."

"Well, you've got a head injury. We're going to find a protected spot and rest. Unless you want to try to jog out of here and kill what few brain cells you still have."

She was slow to catch it, but then she smiled. "Shut up."

———

She sat as close to the fire as she dared, wrapped in Ben's heat-reflecting blanket with a sleeping bag draped around her. The whir and jingle of insects formed a curtain of sound, interrupted occasionally by the soulful call of an owl and the yips of young coyotes.

She was a painful, block of ice. Her head pounded as her rib fought every breath.

"Drink." Ben prodded the fire with a long stick.

It felt like a dozen scorpions had moved into her stomach. But she sipped water, fighting nausea as it cooled her esophagus.

"I don't remember how I ended up in the pond. Well, I think I was scrabbling at the weeds? Under water? I was drowning."

"Look at your hands. They're all cut up."

She lifted a hand. Gashes ribboned her fingers. Her brain flicked around recent memories. The cliff's edge. Roland's knapsack. Thunder? Her stomach twisted. What was going on? She couldn't pull the shreds together.

"Where's Roland?" His tone sounded almost too casual. "Have you seen any sign of him?"

"No." A flash. He was standing nearby? "I don't think so." She couldn't connect the fleeting scraps. "I think someone shot at me. Who is it?"

"Chasing you?"

"Yeah."

He looked away from the fire, his gaze on her. "Where's Roland?"

"What do you mean?"

"I mean, why haven't we found him?"

Her nausea mingled with fear. Was he dead? "What are you saying?"

He unlocked his phone.

"Look. Look at this. Do you remember this?"

She squinted at it. Her focus was off. "That stupid spa. I didn't want to go in."

"What about this?"

"Who is that?"

"It's not you?"

"In a wedding dress? I hardly think so. And we didn't stop at an overlook."

Ben's jaw muscles tightened and relaxed, tightened again. Was he angry?

"What?" She said. "What are these?"

128

He opened the photo of her and Roland showing off the wedding ring. She snorted a chuckle. It looked hilarious. "That's an old photo someone doctored. Weird." Wait. It wasn't funny. She tried to fight the dullness in her head. Why had someone done it? "No. This didn't happen. Where did you find these photos?"

"And this?"

Roland kissing a bride that … looked like her, but slightly off.

She pushed the phone away. "Stop it. What are these?"

"You posted them on your social media."

She might have a concussion, but she was one-hundred percent sure on this. "No. I did not."

"Look closer. It's a screen shot. Your name is right there."

"I didn't post that. That's a lie. Someone's hacked my account."

"And posted this? Why?" His expression and voice were hard.

"Are you accusing me of something? Marrying Roland and denying it, or what?"

His eyes softened. "No! No, not you. Just look. Look at these texts I got from you."

The small print wobbled, but when she finally read it, fury bubbled through everything terrible she was already feeling.

"What the fuck is that? I never sent that. Do you think I'd just write, 'I'm marrying Roland. Sorry! So sad. La-la-la?'"

"No. I don't think that."

She stared into the fire. She wanted to show him something. But what? Why were her thoughts so slow and dumb? Oh, her phone.

"Wait. Look. Here are my texts." A fresh crack ran across the glass, but it was dry in the case. She punched in her password, taking a couple times to get it right. "See? But you were so, I don't know, uninterested."

"Let's see." He took it and scrolled. "No. I didn't get these. What? No, I never saw this text that said when you were coming back, and I certainly wouldn't have been so blah about it."

"Check the number."

"Oh. No. See? This isn't my phone number. It's got my name on it, but it's not mine."

"Let me see. No. That's not Nini's either! I'm not sure if this is Kaitlyn's or not. And where are the rest of my contacts? This is only a few people. You, Kaitlyn, Nini, my shrink, Roland. But that is Roland's actual number. This is so messed up. Hold on."

She popped the phone out of the case and flipped it over. The back was pristine. She held it up to Ben, speechless.

"What? Oh! No scratches!"

"Exactly." She worked her brain hard. "He gave me the case before we left. But I fell asleep in the car. Did he...?"

"Switch your phone? Prevent you from reaching anyone you know?" Ben sounded ferocious.

"And post all that nonsense as me?" She held her aching face. "But why? Why?"

"He faked your marriage. Now..." He shut his mouth tight.

"Now he's trying to kill me?"

He looked into her eyes, brow low, lips a thin line.

Her head pounded. "But why? I don't understand. What could he possibly gain from doing that? Is he trying to make it look like an accident? He wouldn't even get anything. I don't have anything."

"Did he take out a life insurance policy on you?"

"But don't you have to be married to someone to do that? Or do you?"

"I'm not sure."

Images flipped through her thoughts like book pages, landing on the man in the bog, watching her, quiet, as she struggled for air.

"That was him."

"What?"

"He was watching. He didn't help me. I was drowning. I saw him there. I thought…it was someone else. Or that I imagined it. It was just…I was so…"

Rage combined with a deep, painful sadness. Roland really was trying to kill her. Besides the confusion, she was exhausted and aching. "I can't do this. I can't. I have to…"

"You have to rest. Go ahead and get in the tent. I'll watch the fire. Keep that reflective sheet over you, inside the bag."

"No." The voice came from the darkness, making them both look up in shock. "You're taking a walk. Back to the bog."

A dark figure stood shadowed outside the firelight, pointing a pistol.

Chapter 31

KILLING Ash "accidentally" would be a hell of a lot harder with Ben Haus hovering around.

God, why did everything have to be so difficult?

Roland's mouth turned down, icy eyes squinting at the soft firelight, two shapes silhouetted there. He aimed his pistol at the larger one.

"*Pew-pew,*" he whispered.

For kicks, he aimed at the other one.

"*Pew.*"

All this excruciating planning on such a long, winding and goddamned difficult path. It'd be over soon. He'd have all the money. He'd save his son. Or at least, he'd have enough to try every drug, every treatment. If nothing else, they'd go fighting, with the best care anyone on the planet could buy.

Back when he interned with his father, the gorgeous Ash and the trust fund that came with her were an impossible dream. Hell, the last time she'd even acknowledged him, they were just little kids in third grade. Anyway, when he was still an intern, he wasn't desperate for money, so she was just a harmless daydream. Back then, still living with the delusion that he could expect his own, eventual family inheritance, his needs were simpler: He needed a beautiful, intelligent wife who would both love him and be acceptable to his parents. And they expected a cute, roly-poly, white grandchild, the next heir.

But the devastating truth was the women his parents would approve of seemed to regard him as invisible at best, repulsive at worst. His parents always pushed, hooking him up with these pasty pale, silicone-filled country club bitches, but if he made it to one date, it never became two.

Screw that. He was lonely and absolutely could not handle another rejection. Searching, he stumbled into the queasy world of mail-order brides. At first, it was a joke. But the more he looked, the smarter it seemed. There were so many! And they really liked him. But there was that one major obstacle. His parents had certain standards that could not, would not, be bent. They would never tolerate a foreigner, let alone one with dark skin. He'd be cut off in a heartbeat, just to teach him a lesson. Any actions he pursued in that direction had to be kept a tight secret from them.

Well, he happened to be exceptional at strategic games. This was just another one, but life-sized, with game pieces that breathed and moved. Move One, pick a bride. He chose Renata ("I'm a passionate, fun-loving, adventurous, romantic woman who believes in sharing loving time with my partner." Plus, busty, with a brilliant, naughty smile).

Move Two: Get her to the States and hide his parents from her. That was more complicated. He drew out a bunch of alternatives and eventually identified the strongest one. But to make it work, he needed a second identity. He started deep research on the best way to obtain one.

Killing Johnny was an impulse. As soon as he heard the guy lived in a shelter, he realized his opportunity had pedaled right into his web. Nobody would miss some homeless bike courier, disappeared from the vast streets of Chicago. Roland now could build a second existence as John Jameson.

But getting Renata to the US drained his last penny. This new family — Johnny's family — needed so many things. The condo and cars came on credit. His fresh, shiny wife wouldn't stay for long if she figured out he was broke. So, he accepted the HOA fees, a mortgage, car loans. And—surprise!—her parents expected money every month. She claimed it was cultural, but he recognized what it really was: Rent.

He scraped along for a while, borrowing more and more from his parents until they started to pull back. But what really sunk him was his sweet son's hospital bills. And the tantalizing dreams that doctors kept dangling, an exploratory treatment, an experimental medicine. The next one could be the cure. He might buy his son's life if he had enough money.

But then his father got his stupid ass fired after stealing from his clients and offed himself, leaving stacks of gambling debt to Roland and his mother. There was nothing left. Just a life insurance policy that barely covered his mother's expenses. Even today, Roland's dotty mother didn't know they were hanging by a thread. Another secret, another financial burden.

Move Three: Get that trust fund. After sketching out several different ways to steal it, he eventually realized the only safe way to get his hands on it was to marry Ash. Bigamy was nothing in the face of something so critical. A bonus: To his mother, Ash was an ideal choice. But how could he pull it off? He had to get himself in front of her, but would she even notice him?

Finally, fate created the smallest opening. That rafting accident. He heard about it through mutual acquaintances, who added that rumor was that it had left Ash shell-shocked, adrift, looking for anything that promised safety and stability. Time to make his move. He tracked her to college, accepting any work assignments that placed him near there. He found her, reintroducing himself, the son of her father's old business partner, offering his boring stability, with his lucrative future in finance and an apartment in a stodgy neighborhood.

Hallelujah. It worked. The accident had messed Ash up, and he liked her that way, confused and vulnerable. She clung like a koala bear to the safety he offered.

Move Four: Find Nini's other grandchildren. Hello, Graham, the ruthless felon with his own life-threatening money problems. First he told Higman that his family had fled to Mill Valley and the fool raced there, blinded by anger, power and humiliation. Then Roland pulled in Graham to execute the quid pro quo: His grandmother's death and all that money for the whereabouts of Higman's wife and kids. Obviously, Graham couldn't let Higman live after that, so the only connection to Roland, or rather, Johnny, was severed. Then he just had to get rid of Graham. Staging the assassination to seem like a cartel hit was an act of brilliance.

But then, disaster. He heard it in her voice. She was pulling away. Healing or whatever. He'd lose her in a matter of weeks, even days, probably as soon as she returned to Brooklyn. He had to come up with a new plan.

Okay, Roland. It was just a giant Chess board, just keep thinking three moves ahead. He had some time to put the pieces in place, but not much.

Move Five: "Marry" fast and kill her off.

God, his brain ached. Stealing her social security card and passport. Finding a tired, old justice of the peace in a tiny town near Saratoga. Hiring a goddamned call girl to go through that farce of a wedding ceremony and sign the will he forged leaving everything to him. Switching their phones to intercept and respond to her friends. Photoshopping wedding photos so people wouldn't question their marriage.

And after all that, here was aggravating Ben Haus, riding up like some stupid knight to rescue her.

If only she'd died when he shoved her off the cliff. Ben could have found her body. Roland would come stumbling out of the woods, confused and injured, saying she fell in the rain, and he got lost trying to find her.

Now, his exhausted but brilliant brain had to work overtime to devise a way to pull a victory out of this ugly mess.

Move Six: Shoot Ben and drag him into the bog. He'd become another missing person, swallowed by the vast, remote Adirondacks. Bash Ash's head in and leave her at the bottom of a cliff.

Move Seven: Get the money, return to his real wife and save his son.

Nothing would stop him now that he was just three moves from winning the game. Just three moves from collecting the prize.

Chapter 32

ASH launched low like a puma. Her thinking might be addled, but she was sure of one thing: She wanted to hurt Roland for what he'd done.

She hit his knees with a satisfying crunch, even as her broken rib cut her breathing short. He fell sideways, screaming. His pistol fired by her head making her head whir like a snare drum. Her hand clamped against her ear as she kicked Roland's glasses off, both of them flailing, the pistol falling. She clamored for it, but Roland's hand was there first, even before Ben got to them.

"Watch out!" Ben's arms clamped around her legs, dragging her backward. Roland scrambled away, barely aiming, firing again.

Ben fell, clutching his leg. "Ow! You stupid son of a bitch!"

Ash was pure rage as she reached for anything that would hurt him. She found the stick Ben had used to tend the fire and swung it at Roland's head. It connected with a satisfying snap, leaving a red welt on his cheek.

"Jesus!" Roland rolled away, sitting up, pointing the gun at her.

Ben tried to stand. "Ash, no!" he said, teeth clenched.

She roared as she raised the stick, aiming for Roland's nose.

"Stop it! Ash!" Roland swung the pistol at Ben. "Stop or the next bullet will be in his heart."

Fear now surged, quelling her fury. Ben was so close to the gun's muzzle. She dropped the stick and raised her hands. "Okay."

"Jesus Christ! Finally. Go over by him." Roland straightened, rubbing his cheek but still pointing the gun at them. His hand shook—with fear? Tension? Did that make him more likely to pull the trigger or less? "That's right. Stand by your boyfriend, you unfaithful slut."

"What is the matter with you?" She ignored the biteless barb. "Why are you doing this?"

"Just shut up. I'll deal with you in a while. Give me your phones."

"What? Why?" she said.

"Give them to me."

"This isn't even my phone, as you very well know." She threw the phone at his face, forcing him to duck as Ben tossed his on the ground.

"Start toward the bog. Help him up."

Ben pulled himself up on one leg. His pants were torn where the bullet had entered, below his knee. His foot hung limply.

"I can't move it," he said. "It won't flex."

This was bad. She spotted a longer branch and grabbed it.

"Watch it," Roland said. "Drop that."

"It's a crutch, you idiot." She handed it to Ben and put her arm around his waist for support.

"We can't go into the bog in the dark." Ben leaned on the branch. "We'll all fall in."

Roland tossed him a small flashlight. "Use this. Let's go. You first." He nodded at Ash. "If you try to run into the woods, I'll shoot him."

"I'm not going to run, you sickening prick. You…" She tried to think of worse things to call him, but her head was pounding and her thoughts turned to fog.

"Just shut up. Get going."

The deadly bog glowed ahead of them. Entering it at night was insane. When they stepped to its edge in the dim moonlight, she stopped.

"Keep going."

"Where?" Ben said. "One wrong step and we'll sink in. We're right at the edge. We'll all fall through if we keep going."

Ash spun to face Roland, planting her feet. "What are you doing? We can't go in there. We'll all die."

"Keep walking. That way."

"There's twenty feet of water under there," she said.

"If you don't head that way, I'll start shooting."

She had an impulse. Her brain wasn't working fast enough to determine if it was a bad decision. "Help!" she yelled it as loud as she could. "Help!"

"Stop that." Roland hissed. He seemed afraid to get too close to her.

"Help!"

"There's no one who can hear. Stop!"

"Hello! Help! Over here!"

The crack of the gun sounded too close. She ducked, landing on the wiry weeds. Ben fell.

"No!" She scuttled to him, reaching for his face.

"I'm okay. I'm not hit. My stick went through."

They were close to a narrow channel of water. Now she realized what Roland was doing. "He's going to dump us here."

"Not both of you. Just him. I need them to find your body." Roland said. "Keep going, Ben. Go toward the water."

"No, you fucking idiot. Do you think I'm going to make this easier for you?"

"Move or I'll smash her head with a rock. I don't care how she dies as long as it looks like an accident."

"Okay, okay. Hang on. My stick went through. I'm tangled up here." To Ash, he whispered, "As soon as you can, run."

"No. I'm going to kill him before he can hurt us anymore."

"Shh. You're not thinking right. He's got a gun."

139

She'd burst up, fly at him, knock him over, grab the gun. Ash's insides squirmed as her thoughts darted. A rock. Anything that could become a weapon. Ben struggled to free the stick from the tangled weeds. She felt around, her hands finding a good sized rock, plugged in the moss. She fumbled with it, trying to figure out where Roland was without looking back at him.

"Hold on a second," she said, delaying as she tried to decide where to strike. "I'm just trying to help him up."

He didn't answer, so she chattered on. "This stick is really wedged in. Okay, I'm getting it. Hold on." She yanked on the rock.

But why the heck was Roland so quiet? He hadn't spoken for almost a minute. She froze, listening, holding her breath, trying to quiet her heart that pounded so hard. The chorus of crickets and katydids seemed to swell, blanketing all other sounds.

"Ash, don't," Ben whispered.

Squatting, clutching the rock, she looked cautiously around. She expected to see his silhouette against the dark sky. Instead, she saw a lump on the ground.

"Look!" She was up.

"Ash, no!" Ben rolled into a sit. "Oh. What's wrong with him?

She tiptoed to Roland, rock held ready, as Ben hobbled up, shining the light on Roland's prone form. A tingle crept from her tailbone to her neck. Even in the bleaching light, Roland was paler than any human should be. Any living human.

She kicked him in the shoulder. His body jolted, but he didn't respond. "I think he's dead."

Ben reached down toward his neck to find a pulse, but he pulled his hand back, wet with sticky fluid that looked black in the flashlight beam.

"I'd say so."

"But how? What did he do? Stab himself in the neck? What on earth is going on?"

"Maybe somebody else did it?" Ben scanned the edge of the bog. He rubbed his shin. "This burns like a son of a bitch. But I think I'm starting to get movement back."

She squinted through the darkness. "What's that?"

She was sure she saw something quickly moving away, barely visible, a light blur in the black woods.

"What? I don't see it."

"It's ... well, I don't see it now either. I thought it was something moving."

It had been impossible to focus on it, a blob with no defined edges in the darkness, fading in and out among the trees. She wasn't sure she even saw it. And even if she had, there were lots of things moving in the Adirondack woods at night. Probably a deer, or a fox. Or it could be her eyes playing tricks on her as the wind gently blew through the undergrowth in the black trees.

It could be any of those things. It might be nothing.

Okay, that was weird. Her thought processes must really be messed up. Why else would she suddenly start thinking about Graham Novak's fat white dog?

Chapter 33

AT FIRST, Graham had been curious when he spotted Ash's boyfriend coming out of the cheap motel. Was it him? Why was the guy staying in a motel? Why wasn't he at Nini's with Ash? But when he drove past Nini's vacant house, his curiosity morphed into something more urgent. Why was he in town without Ash? Perhaps he'd misidentified him.

He pulled over and scrolled social media, searching for Ash. Her accounts were locked down, tightly private. He checked instead for Ben Haus, finding a list of his friends. Who was that one, a familiar, dark-haired woman with a big grin? He clicked on her, and bingo! This Kaitlyn person's privacy settings were loose, and she had plenty of pictures of Ash with a man. Yes, the same man he'd just seen by the motel. That guy seemed to have no accounts. But he noticed in one photo that he was wearing a dress shirt with a monogram. He zoomed in. "GRC."

His guts prickled. He pulled out quickly, apologizing to Cookie for nearly throwing her off the seat, calling Aldrich as he drove.

"Hey handsome, what's up?"

"My cousin is dating a guy with the initials, 'GRC.'"

"GRC?" Aldrich was silent for a moment. "Oh!"

"Yeah. I'm guessing that George Churchman had a son with the same name. Could that be the "2" in the username, CHUGEO2?"

"Yes. Yes, I would think that's likely. I saw his son mentioned somewhere along the line, but I thought he had a different name? Let's see."

Graham heard clicking.

"Oh, yes! Roland. Well, obviously, he must go by his middle name."

"Check and see if the son works at that financial company."

Graham needed to think, and Cookie needed a walk. After parking in his driveway, he took her straight to the cemetery. He couldn't focus, his thoughts bouncing. He decided he needed to be at home, after all, so he could use his laptop to check a few things. On the way back home, he saw a familiar car slowing by his house. He stepped back behind a thicket of sumac and watched.

Yes, that was Roland Churchman.

Graham should have been a complete stranger to him. He wouldn't have any business with him related to the hardware store where Graham had worked or with meth, and he shouldn't be aware that Graham was Ash's cousin.

Or should he?

His burner rang with Aldrich's number.

"Yeah," he whispered, watching as Churchman's car turned around and passed Graham's trailer a second time before pulling onto the main road.

"Jackpot. G. Roland Churchman 2 interned for three summers at his father's firm. He still picks up work there during busy times, mostly year end and tax time. That would explain his account still being active. Oh, and, by the way, he regularly flies from Tampa to Newark."

Graham made sure Roland's car was gone before crossing the street and entering his trailer.

"So, Ash Harrison's fiancé is going in to view her grandmother's $22 million trust?"

"It appears so."

"And he's regularly flying back and forth from Tampa?"

Graham grabbed a Pepsi and sat down at his laptop.

"Get this. On the days John Jameson parks his car at the Tampa airport, Roland Churchman flies. Usually to Newark. Sometimes LaGuardia."

"And when he gets back to Tampa?"

"John Jameson's car leaves the parking lot and goes back to his condo."

Cookie lapped water from her metal bowl, her collar rattling against it. He got up and refilled her bowl as she settled in her bed with a groan.

"So, what is this telling us?" Graham said. "Is this Churchman guy using Jameson's car? Why is he going back and forth so often?"

"Well, that's a possibility. But I think there's a more likely possibility. Well, more likely in one way, but also completely bizarre in another."

Graham already knew the answer, but he couldn't believe it, even as he said it. "Roland Churchman is John Jameson."

"Yes. I think this man who lives in Tampa with his wife and sick son, the man buried in debt, is the same man that Ash Harrison is planning to marry."

"And if he marries her, he'll have access to that money."

"Well, discounting the fact that it's illegal to have two wives, and assuming that Ash has been named to inherit the trust fund, I would think that would be a pretty easy step for someone who has already come this far."

"At least he can get her half."

"Why just half? Who's getting the other half?"

Something about the way Aldrich asked made Graham suspect he already knew the answer. It wouldn't have been hard for someone like Aldrich to find all the connections during his extensive search.

"I'm guessing it's someone who needs to watch his ass," Aldrich suggested quietly.

"Let me know if you find anything else. And thanks."

Graham looked out the kitchen window. The street was empty.

The man who had driven by his house was not only dangerous, but the biggest threat he faced, bigger than Wyckoff, bigger even than Luis. Of all the people who wanted Graham for something, this one was by far the deadliest.

The caller had said he needed Higman dead. Higman was an oaf, a bully. There was probably a line of people who wished him dead. Graham's accepting the agreement to kill Higman never troubled him. But now, as he looked more deeply at the series of events, he realized he was a pawn in a much bigger story.

The caller didn't want Higman dead. He wanted Nini dead.

For a moment, Graham felt nothing but fury at being tricked into making a decision that resulted in the death of one of his few living relatives. But as he stepped away from his anger, it dawned upon him that the only possible next step for the caller, for Roland, was to dispose of Graham. Kill Graham, and the only other person who knew about Roland's plot to kill Nini and Higman was erased. Kill Graham and Roland's fortune doubled.

And, if he so desired, all that would be next would be to marry and kill Ash. Then he'd go back to his real wife and sick kid a wealthy man. No strings attached.

This guy had outplayed him on every turn, invisible and anonymous. That he now let himself be seen must mean that he didn't expect Graham to realize the danger. Either that, or he didn't care because he intended to make sure that Graham could never expose him or even fight back.

Roland was wrong, on both counts. He made a mistake by letting Graham see him, and Graham hoped it gave him all the time he needed to act. But he must work fast.

Watching out the window, Graham focused on what Roland might plan. Roland knew about the money Graham owed Luis. That gave Roland a convenient reason to execute Graham, Cartel-style. He would come at Graham with a pistol. He couldn't risk being seen, so he would do it in a private place. And he wouldn't risk Graham being able to react, so he would do it when Graham was unaware. Somewhere remote.

That's how Graham would do it.

Where was the proof? He checked his windows. They were all shut and locked, as usual. But this trailer had a back door in its second bedroom, a tiny box Graham barely used. When he turned on the light, he saw it: A semi-circle scuff in the carpet by the door. He found a piece of electrical tape covering the bolt, preventing it from locking.

The hit would come as soon as tonight.

His first impulse was to put a slug in him the minute he entered the back door. But as he considered things, he realized that his own assassination had an incredible upside. Luis could not get money from a dead man. He'd never try to find Graham again. Graham would be free to hunt down Roland unfettered. But he needed a cadaver.

Luckily, he knew where to find one.

Chapter 34

THE dead junkie lay exactly how Graham had left him, slumped on his side on the floor, curled around the leg of the coffee table. The air conditioning kept the small apartment unbearably cold. This delayed his decomposition, but not entirely. The stench was horrendous, the body flaccid and pale, purple along the side resting against the carpet. At least the arms and legs stayed attached as he pulled the corpse onto a tarp and wrapped him tight. He dragged it through the back door and slid it down the outside staircase, guiding it to prevent it from picking up too much speed, then shoved it in his truck.

He tried to squelch the paranoia of driving through town, past hundreds of security cameras on homes, businesses and doorbells, with a wrapped corpse in his truck's open bed. It was the last time he'd use that truck. He had to switch to the cheap Honda he'd just bought with cash.

Nearing his trailer, he scrutinized the surroundings for any sign of Roland. Seeing none, he pulled the junkie inside. He changed the junkie's urine-and-crap-covered clothing for a pair of his own shorts and an undershirt and put him in his bed. It was disgusting, but he'd never sleep there again. Once the corpse lay on his side, back to the door, Graham stepped away, satisfied. Cookie sniffed the body up and down, then backed off, hackles up. She cocked her head at Graham as though awaiting an explanation.

"It's weird, yeah."

Ash had left everything on and connected: Lights, Nini's broadband, heat if he needed it. It was all there to welcome him in a family home he'd never known. The biggest drawback was the mess Ash had left while trying to figure out what to get rid of and what to keep. It looked haphazard, reflecting the cluttered mind of someone deep in hopeless grief.

First things first. He stripped his clothes that stunk of gasoline. He wasn't able to keep it from splashing as he'd dumped it on the cadaver and through the rest of his trailer before setting the whole mess ablaze. Now, he burned them in Nini's outdoor fireplace, then spread the ashes in the weeds.

After a shower, he turned on Nini's laptop and connected to his accounts. The first thing he had to do was warn Ash. Afterward, he'd be smart to leave this town for good. Even Wyckoff wouldn't chase a dead man.

But how cautious did he need to be?

He tried to put himself in Roland's mind. The man was wary and clever. Graham didn't doubt he was watching Ash's accounts somehow and possibly even intercepting communications. Graham wasn't about to cause more trouble for Ash, and he couldn't tip Roland off to the fact that he, Graham, was still alive. He needed more information, and for that, he needed Aldrich. But it was 3 a.m. Even Aldrich had his limits.

His head felt stuffed with wet towels. He found a sleeping bag in an upstairs closet and curled up on Nini's bed, Cookie already snoring on a thick, wool blanket he'd laid on the floor. He tried to enumerate the things he would do when he awoke, but after thirty seconds, his thoughts switched off and he was sound asleep.

He jerked alert with the fear that he was running out of time.

"Hey buddy," he typed to Aldrich. "Got a sec?"

"Always."

Graham called him. "I think this Roland Churchman is going to hurt my cousin. I need your mad skills."

"Okay, I'm all yours. What's today's plot?"

"I want to try to warn her, but he's smart enough to be watching her accounts. Is there any way you can check her phone to see if it's been hacked?"

"Hmm, that's both scary and interesting," Aldrich said. "What's her number?"

Graham gave it to him.

"Okay, let me see if I can find anything funny going on with it. I'll let you know."

While he was waiting, Graham explored Nini's house and found her photo albums. In the early ones, when Nini was married, he saw pictures of his grandfather for the first time. The man was lean and sinewy, and Graham's resemblance to him was striking. He found boyhood photos of his own father, never smiling, often immaturely making faces at the camera.

An envelope, tucked in the pages, dropped to his lap. He recognized his mother's erratic scrawl. He found his own baby photo folded in a letter telling Nini of Graham's existence and pleading for money.

Graham snorted, knowing that any money Nini might have sent would have gone into his mother's arm or up her nose. But he found two unopened letters to his father in jail, marked, "Refused." He opened them and started reading. Nini had tried to contact his father after Graham was born, asking for confirmation that the baby was his, and if so, asking to meet him. His father had refused to even read the letters.

How might his life have been different if his father had introduced him to Nini when he was a boy instead of lurking up in the woods? They had been so near. If he'd known Nini, he might've had a safe place to stay when his mother disappeared for weeks. Warmth. Food.

Aldrich's call halted his brooding.

"Okay. Her phone appears to be okay, but it is in a remote place. It looks to be a heavily wooded area in the Adirondack Park, which looks beautiful, by the way. We don't have anything like that where I am."

"Where abouts?"

"I'm in Kansas."

"No, the phone."

"Oh. Ha. My mistake. I'll give you the coordinates, because it's not very close to any town. The nearest bigger town is Saranac Lake." He gave them to Graham. "I had to use the satellite because there is no cell there. Your messages probably won't get through."

Graham considered. "Two more things. We need to know where our bigamist is. And hold on." He did a quick search for Ben Haus' backwoods outings website and found his cell number. "And can you tell me the whereabouts of this cell number? Oh, and can we follow these numbers every couple of hours?"

"Boy, you're really adding to your debt."

"When this is over we can spend a month playing Super Mario or Monopoly or whatever you want."

"That will work." Aldrich was quiet, then said. "You know what would be really helpful?"

"What?"

"A drone. It's so big up there. She could be lost and anyone trying to find her could also get lost. If we find a drone pilot up in that area, he could send a camera out to see what's going on. Maybe he could spot Ash."

"Know any?"

"I might. I'm a member of a lot of drone clubs. Let me see who we can find."

"You're pure geek, aren't you, dude?"

"I told you a long time ago how helpful I can be."

When Aldrich called back and told him that Ben was already near Saranac Lake, Graham felt a surge of hope. He wanted to warn Ben and Ash, but he couldn't let them figure out his disastrous relationship with Roland. If they were aware of his involvement, they might eventually connect him to Nini's death. So, he kept his text to Ben anonymous.

"This is Ash's last location. Get there fast."

He sat back with a sigh. Cookie groaned, stood, stretched and lay back down, tucked against his leg.

Time to let it go. He'd done what he could. It was time to trust Ben to find Ash and get her out of there safely. He didn't need to haul his ass up to some Adirondack bog and get in the middle of things. What he did need to do was take advantage of his own death and get out of here, away from Wyckoff, away from a chance sighting by the Rochester cartel. Away from the one guy who wanted him to be and stay dead, Roland Churchman. He was free to go anywhere, start again anyplace in the world. He still had most of Jory's cash. That was enough to go on for a while. He'd go to Texas, work on a rig. Or maybe drive an 18-wheeler across the country until he found a place where he might like to live.

He was truly free for the first time. The world opened, arms wide, welcoming him to anything he wanted to do.

But Roland Churchman was out there. And he was deadly.

If Ash was wandering around in a bog, where was that guy? He probably still had the gun he'd used at Graham's. Would he kill her, just as fast and cold as he put bullets in that corpse? Or would he live out the lie for longer, play house with Ash as if he didn't have a second family?

He wondered how much she knew now, if she was still with him or fleeing from him. Why was she in the middle of nowhere?

And what about Ben? Graham might send him straight into an ambush.

Goddamnit. Sure, the world was open to him now, and he could do anything he wanted. He'd escape, leave everything behind and start a new life. That's what he wanted. He should go. Let them figure it out.

But if he didn't save Ash, he'd have no life. He would hate himself forever.

And as far as what he wanted, really wanted, deep down in his soul?

Two things: He wanted Nini back, an impossible, desperate longing. And he wanted to kill Roland Churchman, making sure the monster realized who did it. That he could do, or at least try.

Graham would not have a life anywhere else until he settled things here.

Well, hell.

"Let's go, girl."

Ben would find Ash. Graham was hunting a more dangerous game.

Chapter 35

GRAHAM sat in a Tupper Lake McDonald's, awaiting a report. Aldrich had quickly found a local drone pilot, who sent a camera up over the bog. Thoughts buzzing, he scrolled through the news. A headline sent a tingle up his neck: "Suspected Cartel Boss Lazcanos Assassinated in Rochester Home."

Could it be true? Was the major source of his daily terror gone like smoke in the clouds?

He checked a couple more sources. Yes, true. A tremendous weight lifted from his psyche.

He was never this lucky. And that wasn't the only extraordinary thing going his way. Assuming Ben found Ash first, Wyckoff would learn about Roland's scheme to kill Nini for her money, knock off Graham and marry Ash. That could only be good for Graham.

Relief flooded him, but his stomach lurched. He didn't need the money now. If he'd just waited a few weeks, Nini would still be alive.

His phone rang, Aldrich. He cleared his throat and refocused. "Hey, what did he find?"

"She's in a bad spot, possibly trapped in a scary thing called a bog pond. Apparently, you can't get out of this type of pond. Something about the edges are springs or something? I really didn't understand the man, frankly. Apparently, I don't speak Backwoodsman, even when they're on the geeky side."

"Okay."

"And there are two other people in the vicinity. Men. One is walking sort of toward her, but apparently, it's very difficult walking, and he's not exactly on the right path. The other is at the edge of the woods, near this bog pond and not moving very much. Do they sound like your guys?"

"They do, yes. Here, let me pull it up." He found a map online and scrolled around the satellite view. I think I see the pond. Is it in the southwest corner?"

"Yes, that's right."

"How far is the moving one from Ash?"

"Oh, he's meandering her way. If he's lucky and doesn't fall through, he should run into her within half an hour, our pilot guessed."

"But the other one is just hanging out? Do you think he can see Ash?"

"We don't know, but it's interesting that he's not attempting to help her, if he can. Almost as if he's waiting for her to drown, if you get my gist."

"What else you got?"

"The pilot notified the local search and rescue, as you suggested," Aldrich said. "But it'll take them some time to mobilize. Apparently, there was a flash flood up in one of the rivers, and it swept through a canyon swimming hole so quickly that people didn't have time to get out. So now all the responders from all the nearby towns are up there. In fact, my drone pilot is heading up there to fly over to find anyone underwater. I really think I changed my mind about wanting to visit the Adirondacks, between the lethal moss and this problem with the swimming facilities."

"Thanks again."

"What are you going to do?"

"I'm heading into the lethal moss."

Graham hurried through the woods bordering the bog, heading south, Cookie on her leash. He followed Aldrich's coordinates, leaving the woods and reaching the pond at dusk. No surprise that Ash was not in the water, but whether she'd been rescued or drowned, he didn't know. His heart sputtered with anxiety as the sun sunk low.

Okay, where would I go if I had pulled a woman from a bog pond?

Certainly not back through the bog. Ben was like him: He was good in the woods. He would take Ash to the safety of solid ground and the thick cover of trees, where there would be protection from weather and potential hiding places if necessary. Graham had come in from the north, but civilization also lay to the south, almost equidistant. He'd try it. Darkness was coming fast, but if they had a fire, it would be easier to find them than in the daytime.

Their fire was still burning, but where were they? Graham poked through the scant belongings by the tent. The light backpack held few items, but smart ones, made for survival in the wild. This had to be Ben's. And this jacket hanging near the fire to dry was the right size for Ash. He examined it, noting the many tears and dark, reddish-brown stains. He looked around, listening. It was damned near impossible to hear anything except the riotous buzz of insects and trill of frogs. Cookie gazed toward the bog, her nostrils twitching. Maybe she couldn't hear them, either, but she had a tool he didn't: her great sense of smell. He looked that way, seeing nothing but the black shape of trees and shrubs against the slightly grayer blackness of the bog.

Was that a shot? The crack was buffered by the vast woods and the insect song.

Then he heard it, a thin cry, lifted along the cool night breeze, rising above the other sounds. And again, definitely a "Help."

As he pulled his ski mask down, he unsnapped the sheath of his hunting knife, slipping silently that way, his eyes slowly focusing on a shape that could only be a human, standing just inside the bog. And was that...? Yes. Two others, on the ground. In a few fast strides, their features were clear enough so he could tell who each was, and that the object in Roland's hand was a pistol. Graham had no time to plan or evaluate, and he didn't need it.

Go time.

Three more steps and he was behind Roland. In one, quick, well-placed motion, he pressed his hand over Roland's mouth and yanked his chin back as he jabbed the knife into his soft neck, straight into the carotid artery.

Roland's eyes opened wide as he clutched his throat. Graham kept his hand pressed over his mouth as he dropped. He'd be unconscious in less than a minute, then dead, his blood spurting into the moss. Graham should go, but, first, he squatted, peeling back his ski mask, pushing his face close to Roland's until he saw the recognition flicker in his dimming eyes.

"Game over, asshole."

Then Graham pulled Cookie into a quick jog, slipping away in the darkness until he was just another shadow swaying in the gentle woods.

Chapter 36

HIS cell rang with an upstate area code. "Wyckoff."

"Scott? That you?"

"Yeah. Who's this?"

"I don't know if you remember me. It's Jackie Dunlavey. We were in a search and rescue workshop together a few years ago."

"Oh! Okay." He vaguely remembered a sturdy, cheerful, dark-haired, park police officer. "How've you been?"

"Oh, I'm fine thanks. I'm calling because I have a couple of people you might know. Ash Harrison and Ben Haus. They're telling me a wild story."

"Really? Like what?"

"They say her fiancé shoved her off a mountain and chased her through a bog, then held them at gunpoint until someone unknown stabbed him in the neck."

"The fiancé, you say?" How in holy hell had he missed the fact that Ash was engaged? She didn't mention it once. "What's the fiancé's name?"

"Uh, let's see. Roland Churchman. We haven't been able to find his body. They weren't very sure about their location when it happened, and it's a damned big bog. Not to mention scavengers. Anything you can tell me about this bunch?"

"I led an investigation into her grandmother's death as well as … well, it's complicated. But she's not a suspect."

"Gotcha. I mean, she's nice enough, but her story is just wild. But she's got a concussion, among other things, so I don't know. The hospital is keeping her. Ben was shot in the leg."

"Good god. Well, I'll tell you something that makes it wilder. She's inheriting eleven million dollars from her grandmother, and honestly, I don't even think she knows it. I just found out myself."

"Well, that makes it even more interesting, doesn't it? Okay. I guess I'll keep trying to make heads or tails of this. I'll call you if I need anything."

Wyckoff hung up and swung his chair to his computer, entering "Roland Churchman" into the police database. George Roland Churchman. A junior. The guy was clean. No arrests. Not even any traffic tickets. Downright boring.

But if he was so boring, why was Ash claiming he'd chased her through the wilderness, trying to kill her?

"Reggie?"

He found her folding their endless quantity of tiny toddler shirts, pants and pajamas and stuffing them in drawers.

"I think I might have just solved Nini Harrison's murder."

"Again?"

"She has a fiancé."

"Well, well. That wily old lady."

"No, wise guy. Ash. Here I've been trying to pin this thing on Graham. Well, I mean, Higman physically did it, but I thought Graham was behind it. But what if it's been this fiancé all the time? And you know that hit on Graham and the trailer fire?"

"Yeah?" She shut a drawer and pushed hair off her forehead. She was barely listening, he could tell, but it didn't matter.

"I've been blaming the cartel. But what if it was this Roland guy all along? I mean, he might have wanted Graham dead, if he wanted all of Nini's money."

"Dude! You're brilliant." She kissed him as she squeezed past, the half-full laundry basket on her hip.

"No. I'm not. I'm a dumbass."

"Excuse me, but I would not marry a dumbass." She disappeared into their bedroom.

Until he could properly interview Ash, Wyckoff was at a standstill.

Inflamed and frustrated, he took a drive. It was so clear, yet those loose ends aggravated him. Who shot Higman? Why didn't the firefighters find the remains of that gravy boat? And where the heck was Cookie?

He ended up on the road where Graham's trailer had been. A massive bulldozer roared there, dumping debris into a twenty-foot-long, waste container. He watched as the machine lifted the charred foundation of the trailer, backed up, accompanied by shrill beeping, and dumped the frame into the container with a wretched screech and boom.

Who the heck hired this guy? He approached the machine, looking at the operator. He thought he was seeing things. The recently deceased Graham glanced at him but didn't stop, swinging the dozer around again for another load.

He huffed out a sigh, shaking his head, unable to suppress a smile. Why was he so glad to see this sneaky jerk? As his surprise wore off, anger grew. Graham dumped the load and Wyckoff held up his hands to stop him. Graham braked the machine and turned down the RPMs.

"You're going to get hurt doing that." Graham had to yell, despite the now somewhat quieter engine rumble.

"Come on down."

Graham climbed off, followed, of course, by the white dog, who jumped to the cab floor then to the caterpillar tread before walking back and forth on it, looking for a way down. Graham lifted her gently to the ground, and she came up to Wyckoff and touched his pant leg with her nose with a slow, tail wag before wandering onto the lawn.

Leaning against the massive piece of equipment, Graham pulled out his cigarettes. Looking at Wyckoff the whole time, he lit one and blew smoke out the side of his mouth. The odor from the tobacco and the burned building combined with diesel fumes.

"You're interrupting my work, so why don't you get on with whatever it is you want so I can get back to it?"

"Who is the body?"

"What body?"

"The charred pile of bones we found in your bedroom with bullet holes in his skull and spine."

Graham's expression didn't change. "Someone was in my bedroom when the place burned? That's weird. Who was it?"

"Where were you that night?" The engine rumble was a throbbing irritant.

"Black Creek."

"And what, pray tell, is Black Creek?"

"State forest up in Herkimer."

Wyckoff looked at him in silence, but he'd learned long ago that extended silence didn't bother Graham. He just smoked and looked back at Wyckoff, waiting.

"What for?"

"Black bear."

"Black bear." This was going to be a tall tale.

"Hunt starts next month."

"And you went there without your cell phone and without your truck?"

"That against the law?"

"No, but it's pretty strange, isn't it? It's as though you wanted to make it seem like you were in the house when someone shot the person in the bed and set the place on fire. How did you get there?"

Graham nodded at the Honda Accord parked on the lawn.

"Oh, that's a great bear hunting vehicle."

"I was scouting. Hunting would be illegal until September."

"And you wouldn't want to break the law, right?"

Graham rubbed his hands over his face. Wyckoff noticed the dark circles under his red eyes. "You look exhausted."

"Anything else?"

"Why did you leave your phone behind?"

"I wanted some peace."

"Did anybody see you while you were there?"

"I don't know."

"Did you stop for gas?"

"No."

"Food?"

"No."

"You're telling me you drove, what's that, maybe, two-hundred miles round trip and never stopped for gas or food?"

"Right."

"How long were you there?"

"Couple days."

"What did you eat?"

"Sandwiches and chips."

"Motel?"

"Boondocked."

"And you came back and found your house burned to the ground?"

"Yup."

"Where have you been staying?"

"Around."

Wyckoff shook his head in frustration. "I have the urge to arrest you just because you're so annoying."

"That illegal now?"

"What do you know about the person who was in the fire?"

"Nothing."

"Who do you know who might have gone into your house and stayed in your bed while you were away?"

"No one."

"How do I know you didn't shoot this person and set the house on fire yourself?"

"Why would I do that?"

The answer came to Wyckoff in a flash. The look of realization must have shown in his expression because Graham's eyes hinted concern.

"So, whoever was after you would think you were dead."

This brought a rare smile to Graham's thin mouth, and a little snort of amusement.

"Okay, Sherlock. Now, do you mind? I have to get this thing back soon."

"Where'd you get it from?"

"Borrowed it from the town."

"Again? Does the town know you borrowed it?"

"Of course." Graham whistled for the dog and helped her back into the cab. He climbed up behind her and revved up the huge engine, drowning out all possibility of further questions.

Back at his office, Wyckoff found a coroner's report on his desk. Good! It had to be about the body in the trailer. But it contained only a note that said, "Call me."

Katherine, the coroner, picked up on the third ring.

"Hey, Scott."

"Hey. You finished the burn victim?"

"Well, yes and no. That's why I wanted to talk to you. I can tell you for sure that this person was dead before the fire started."

No surprise there, with all those bullet holes.

"Unfortunately, the body burned in hot temperatures for long enough to make identification difficult. He was male, and I was able to collect intact DNA, but so far there is no match. That eliminates the homeowner, Graham Novak. We have his DNA on file since he's a felon."

"Not to mention the fact that I was just talking to him."

"Oh, really? Okay, well then, I can confirm your suspicion that the body was not his." She chuckled. "Did he have any information about this body?"

"Nothing that I could get out of him."

"Okay, well, here's where it gets interesting."

"Yeah?"

"Yeah. I was able to get some data from the liver. Number one, this guy carried a high content of methamphetamine. As in, extreme overdose level."

"That is interesting."

"Number two, he was dead before the bullets entered his body."

Wyckoff's scalp tightened. "Okay."

"In fact, he was dead for days before he was shot."

His surprise left him silent.

"His liver shows evidence of putrefaction. He was already decaying before the bullets penetrated his spine. Likewise, the entry wound in the brain. There is no indication of fresh tissue damage at that location. Someone shot bullets into a dead man. It's a little confusing, though, because the amount of decay is contradictory. It's almost as though the body was refrigerated."

"What?" Each of the scenarios racing through Wyckoff's mind was more outlandish than the next.

"I'm going to send the liver and brain to the state for a second opinion. I've never seen anything like this. But results will not be fast. As in, months, maybe five, six months if we're lucky."

Wyckoff ran his hand through his hair. As frustrating as the situation was, it was also fascinating, and he wanted answers.

When he got back to Graham's place, all the remains of the house were in the waste container and the bulldozer was gone. So, of course, was Graham.

Chapter 37

ASH awoke to a refreshing sensation: No headache. She gazed around at the pale, yellow walls of the motel cabin she and Ben had selected after her release from the hospital four days ago. The hospital had kept her one night and discharged her with painkillers she would not take and a warning to limit her activity for a few days. Ben's calf was stitched where the bullet had ripped through muscle, grazing nerves but fortunately missing bone.

After that insane night in the woods, they'd hiked slowly for hours before reaching a paved road. Exhausted, they sat on the guardrail and waited. Ben waved down the first car they saw, a park ranger's truck. The ranger didn't seem to know what to make of their explanation.

This adorable cabin was comfortable for her convalescence. One of ten on the property, it was a box containing a single room with a bed, its metal frame painted bright green. A tiny bathroom held a shower, sink and toilet and a black and white photograph of men in tall boots and suspenders, holding poles and standing a century ago on logs in some nearby waterway. Cell service and Wi-Fi were iffy. For Ash, it was a perfect choice for healing after her near-fatal run through the wilds.

Ben tried to make himself small in the double bed to avoid bumping her while she healed. Their nights had been all about rest and sleep—so far. His warm back pressed against hers and the katydids song brought back so many comforting memories of camping with him when they were children, snuggled together as they imagined all kinds of scary animals and evil maniacs circling their tent in the blackness of the backyard.

But they were no longer children. And the evil maniacs were real.

As she rolled over, she reached out and found his side empty. She sat up and stretched as he came through the door with coffee. He grinned.

"How are you feeling?"

"My headache's gone!"

He sat on the side of the bed, causing her to slide against him on the squishy mattress. He pushed a wandering curl off her forehead, smiling. She smiled back and then, following a warm impulse, kissed him. He kissed back and looked at her with a wild gleam.

"Oh, really?"

She kissed him again. He rolled onto her, his arms around her, pulling her tight so it felt like every part of his strong self wrapped around her as he kept the kiss going.

"Oof! My rib!"

Their lovemaking was fun, sometimes silly, and gratifying. As the morning tumbled into afternoon, they lay quiet, sleepiness settling in.

"I can't believe this is really happening," she murmured.

"It's about damn time."

She laughed and drifted off to sleep, full of rare, giddy joy.

Chapter 38

ASH thudded up the carpeted stairs of the old Victorian house that held Nini's lawyer's office. Scabs marred her cheek, jaw, neck, chest and hips from her scraping along the cliff. Her broken rib made every movement painful. The concussion was healing, but fast motion still brought pain, and her balance was shaky.

Why didn't she just receive a copy of Nini's will from the lawyer?

In the days that followed her escape from the Adirondacks, Ash had tried to put together the pieces of Roland's lie. She declined Wyckoff's requests to talk but sent him everything. He was smart. He'd figure it all out. She wasn't sure she wanted to hear the full extent of Roland's strategy. But she'd have to speak to Wyckoff eventually, because there was one question she needed answered.

Why?

It made no sense. He must have thought there was real value in being her supposed widower, but she couldn't think of a reason good enough to make him go to such extremes. Certainly, she wasn't worth much dead.

She turned the ornate, brass knob and stepped into the waiting room. It had once been a bedroom of a 19th-century home. Now, it contained cushioned, straight-back chairs and a coffee table bearing large, hardcovered books of photographs. An open doorway to the right allowed an admin to see visitors enter.

But the décor wasn't what caught Ash's attention. What surprised her was the man sitting in one of the corner chairs, scrolling through his phone. He looked up when she entered.

Graham Novak. His gaze showed interest, and possibly, a flash of alarm before he nodded a silent greeting.

"Hi," she said. He'd cut his hair since she saw him last, getting rid of the long, straight bangs and the scraggly length. It was stylish and businesslike. Between that and the new, light gray, short-sleeved button down, navy chinos and smart, tan, leather shoes, she might not have recognized him. The new look flattered his angular face and riveting eyes. She once considered his intelligent gaze to be street smart. Now his somber depth reminded her of the chemistry students she knew back in college. Oddly, his change made him seem more familiar.

He looked away quickly and so did she. What was he doing here, anyway? She popped her head into the admin's door and said, "I'm Ash Harrison, here for the 10:30."

"Oh, good, Ms. Harrison. We're all ready. You can both come in."

"Both?"

"You and Mr. Novak, yes. Right this way." She opened the door to an office. "They're here."

Ash followed her, glancing again at Graham who came behind her. He looked at her uncomfortably, holding the office door for her.

"Good morning." The lawyer was around sixty, chubby and pink-faced, his small, blue eyes peering over reading glasses as he shook their hands. "I'm Louis Petrie. I've been retained as the executor for your grandmother. Please, have a seat."

Ash sat in one of the leather chairs.

"I'm sorry, but I'm confused." She looked from the lawyer to Graham.

"Oh, I'm sorry. Have you not met?"

"Yes, I mean, yes. But why? What?" She didn't know how to ask the question without seeming rude, but this hardware store man at Nini's will reading was too strange.

"Oh, good. That's good. Sometimes these things bring together people who don't even know they're related."

"Related?" Ash looked again at Graham, her confusion growing. He sat in the chair next to hers, glanced at her, looked away and back. He did not appear surprised.

"What is going on?"

"Oh, I see," Petrie said. "We seem to have one of those situations right now. Let me introduce you properly. Ash Harrison, this is your cousin, Graham Novak. Graham, say hello to your cousin, Ash."

"My cousin?" Ash's head throbbed as her blood pressure rose. "I don't have a cousin. My father was an only child!"

"Well, that's how it appeared, yes," Petrie said. "But that wasn't reality. Reality is that she had a second son, David, your father's older brother. He was sent away when he was a teen and led a life separate from his mother and brother." His gaze softened on her. "And from you. Your grandmother had her own reasons for keeping this information from you, but when she learned there might be another grandchild in the mix, that is, your cousin here, she made sure that her will reflected that you both should be inheritors upon her death."

Ash didn't care about sharing the inheritance. What she cared about was that she suddenly had a relative, and, apparently, she was the last to know.

"Is this true?" She stared at Graham. "You knew?"

"For a little while." His expression carried no emotion.

"Well, why in the hell didn't you tell me?"

His shrug was barely perceptible.

"Oh! Now I know! You look like my grandfather."

Graham's right eyebrow lifted, his eyes revealing nothing. Petrie paused to see if Graham would respond, and, when he didn't, continued. "Well, I suppose you two will have a lot to talk about, but shall we proceed with the will?"

Ash's mind raced with questions, and she could barely focus on the lawyer's words. She heard that the estate was to be divided between the two of them, including Nini's real estate, possessions and all financial accounts. Petrie's assistant now handed her and Graham thin folders. She felt a renewed grief. She only wished she still had Nini, alive and loving, sitting in her comfy chair, working through a crossword, looking up with joy when Ash walked in.

"You'll see that the latter-mentioned financial accounts are not insignificant." Petrie nodded at the folders.

The top paper showed a list of numbers, divided in two, with a final sum showing what Ash assumed was her half. She wondered if the concussion was affecting her ability to read. It was like in a dream where the figures refused to make sense.

"How much is here?" Her tone rang high with disbelief. This couldn't be right.

"Your grandmother had about $600,000 in dividend stocks. Between that, social security and a small pension, this was enough to provide her a comfy living in retirement. She never touched the money in the trust. That's the larger amount you see there. For you each, it comes to just over eleven million dollars. Her aunt, your great aunt, was a shrewd investor. She backed oil development in Texas before anyone realized how big it would be. Then she put her returns in blue chips. Time did the rest."

"Eleven million? Dollars?"

"Invested smartly over the past one-hundred years."

The entire experience, from Graham being unexpectedly identified as her cousin to the amount of the inheritance, was too much. Her stomach roiled. She shut the folder, needing to move. She stood, intending to go to the window and steady her thoughts. But her legs refused to cooperate, and blackness crossed her vision as pain jolted her side. It was as if she'd stepped into a hole. She fell.

Strong hands caught her, guiding her to the chair. When she opened her eyes, Graham squatted next to her, brows low.

"Here, Ms. Harrison, drink this." The admin offered a glass of water.

She drank and looked again at Graham.

"Thanks," she said.

His calm eyes warmed. "Got your back."

Chapter 39

As they walked down the office stairs, she wanted to ask him so many questions, learn more about this unexpected relative who had been right there, yet unseen. But he was so stony she didn't know how to start. Plus, she was lost in a haze of confusion and disbelief. Too much had happened. She had no voice.

Maybe he'd come have pizza with her and Ben. She started to ask but a familiar voice interrupted, calling her name. Wyckoff leaned against his car. Graham stopped walking and hung back, eyeing Wyckoff like he was a giant cockroach and reaching for his cigarettes.

"Well, look at you, all cleaned up. I'd have thought you were going to a job interview, but with all that money, now, I know better."

How irksome. "What, does everyone know all these secrets but me?"

"I do have some things to tell you," Wyckoff said. "Care to come to my office?" He nodded to Graham. "Both of you."

"No, thanks." Graham started down the sidewalk. Damn. Wyckoff had chased him off.

"I think you're going to want to hear this, too, Graham."

That was her chance. "I'm meeting Ben for lunch, down at the corner. Can we talk there?"

Graham stopped, sighed, his hard eyes shifting from her to Wyckoff and then back. Sheesh. He was as hard to coax as a feral cat. "Yeah. Okay."

The pizza parlor walls were rustic red bricks. The comforting scents of garlic and yeast set her stomach rumbling. But whether it was from hunger or nausea, she couldn't tell. Her thoughts seemed locked in shock. Too much new information.

"Oh? What's all this?" Ben stood in surprise at the three of them approaching as the server delivered a hot pizza to the table. Wyckoff and Graham shook hands with Ben.

"More plates?" the server asked.

"I guess so," Ben said, eyeing the pizza. He put a slice on a plate for Ash and helped himself to one. His eyes on her were full of questions. She gave him an "I don't know" gesture. So much raced through her mind. The money. All that money, out of nowhere. And a cousin, this cagey guy bearing an uncanny resemblance to her grandpa.

Wyckoff sat next to her, Graham across.

"Well, help yourselves, I guess," Ben said.

Nobody else took any.

"This is one of the more unusual parties I've accidentally hosted." Ben's smile was sweet as he lifted a hand and let it drop.

"You got that right," she mumbled.

"You doing okay? Eat. You don't look so good. What happened?"

"I'm guessing you had a couple shocks," Wyckoff said. "You met your cousin and learned that you're now a rich woman, yes?"

Ben looked from Wyckoff to Graham. "What?"

It was so much. Why didn't Nini spend it on herself? She could have gone around the world, bought a second home in a place where it didn't rain all summer. What was Ash going to do with it? Was it even real?

"Well, I have more info that is going to surprise you. So, yes, you might want to eat because you're definitely not looking great."

The cheese oozed off the edges of her slice, tempting. But her insides were tight. "I fainted in the lawyer's office."

"Can we take a breath here?" Ben rested his hand on her back. "Eat your lunch. Whatever Detective Wyckoff has to say can wait until you get something in your stomach. You, too." He slid a slice onto the plate in front of Graham, and another on Wyckoff's. "Let's just eat, before it gets cold."

"It does look good. Thanks." Wyckoff took a bite. "Go ahead, Graham. Might as well. One big, happy family, right?"

When everyone had finished, Wycoff cleared his throat, his gaze on Ash. She saw he was preparing to say something hard.

"Glad you're sitting down for this," he said. "Here goes. Roland Churchman had a second life, a wife in Florida and a terminally ill son."

Ash heard but barely comprehended. A surprised laugh huffed through her nose before the terrible truth sunk in.

"And he was very familiar with your Nini's trust fund, and who would be inheriting it."

Saliva flooded her mouth, tasting like blood, and she almost puked the slice back up.

"What in holy hell are you talking about?" Ben's hand was on her back again.

"He was playing a long game, Ash. I think he'd been planning this for years. When he learned Higman was seeking his runaway wife and child in Mill Valley, the opportunity to move things forward finally presented itself. If he could find the wife and child, he could use them as leverage to get Higman to kill your grandmother. He was successful, unfortunately. Then he had to kill Higman, of course, which was accomplished on the hill before Marco went over the cliff."

174

The shock burst from Ash. "Are you saying Roland was up there that day? He shot Higman?"

"Possibly." Wyckoff side-eyed Graham. "And he thought he took care of you, too, the night of your house fire." Wyckoff let his gaze stay a little too long on Graham, who frowned and fiddled with a water glass.

"House fire?" Ash vaguely remembered reading about one recently.

"That left just two more things for him to do. Marry you, Ash, and then, presumably, kill you. At that point, he would have the money. He wrote you a new will to ensure that, of course."

"He what?" Infuriating. "He can't do that."

"But why would he have to kill her?" Ben asked. "He could get at the money with her alive."

"Good question. My best guess is he didn't want to maintain such a huge lie, long-term. He was juggling a lot of swords. Without Ash, Johnny Jameson could go back to them, unincumbered. That's his alias. He got it from a bike courier who disappeared a few years ago in Chicago." He watched Ash as it sunk in.

What was he saying? Did Roland do something to that courier?

Wyckoff went on. "He'd use the money to try to save the boy's life, as well as support his mother. But it was folly. The boy's disease is incurable. No amount of money can save him."

Ash's throbbing brain refused to take many more surprises. This was a woozy nightmare.

"But after all the careful planning, what he ended up doing seems uncharacteristically sloppy," Wyckoff was saying. "Pretending to marry you at the justice of the peace? Why do that in such a hurry when you were planning to be married, anyway? After so much calculation, why change this critical thing at the last minute?"

It hit her like a cannon ball. "Because I told him I was breaking up with him."

"Ah, that's what I was wondering. That was the missing piece I expected. So, he had to hurry. He couldn't risk losing you. We're not sure who the woman was he used as a stand-in for you during the ceremony."

Ash's heart pattered, her breathing tight. This couldn't be happening. Roland couldn't have done these things. Wait. He really couldn't have.

"But he was with me. He didn't know I was breaking up with him until I got back to Brooklyn. How could he possibly do these things when he was with me?"

"Was he?" Wyckoff watched her steadily. "Was he with you the Wednesday night before you went to the Adirondacks?"

"Yes. That was the day I returned to Brooklyn. He suggested the trip, right after he got back from Boston."

Wyckoff raised his eyebrows, waiting, watching as it hit her.

"Oh." Her voice squeaked and her face tingled as the true depth of his lies sunk in. "He didn't go to Boston, did he? He went to kill my cousin."

No one said anything.

"But wait, then we went on the trip. How could he do all this…this getting married and signing wills and all that?"

"Good question." Wyckoff took another bite, chewing with his eyes on her. "Did he leave you at any point?"

"No. Not until he left the car when it broke down." Had he rigged the car trouble, too?

"Did he go into the spa with you?" Ben asked.

"No. That's true. For almost four hours he was playing…he said he was playing golf."

"Almost four hours." Wyckoff gazed over her head. "That was Thursday. Okay, that aligns. We know he married the phony Ash that day in Northfield Junction, about a twenty-five minute drive. If he had the girl waiting nearby, that would be more than enough time to get married, sign a will and then…" He refocused on Ash. "Well, we'd love to talk to her. But honestly, I'm not hopeful we'll find her, given his record."

"You mean, he killed her too?" Ben asked.

She could almost smell how fresh and clean Roland was when he picked her up after the spa. Her face grew hot. He killed that woman, then calmly took a shower? She shrunk into her chair, barely able to focus on the conversation. She didn't want to know, didn't want to hear anything more.

"It seems likely, and considering where he was, I think the chances of our finding the body are very low. We're just hoping she's alive and will come forward. And even though he had to change plans at the last minute, it was still ingenious. Swapping phones with you, Ash, appropriating your social media. Intercepting and responding to messages from Ben and your other friend. He would have had to arrange things with the woman he hired at least some time in advance, a few days, at a minimum. He must have known something was up with you, Ash. Quite amazing, really. One thing I haven't heard yet, though. How did you find her in the bog, Ben?"

"I got a message." Ben pulled out his phone and showed him the text. "I don't know who it's from. I didn't even know if I could trust it, but I really didn't have any choice."

Wyckoff took the phone, reading the message. "Unknown number? Interesting." He turned toward Graham. "Interesting, right?"

"Interesting," Graham said, not sounding interested at all as he nibbled the last cheesy sauce from the edge of his pizza crust.

Why did Wyckoff keep looking at Graham like that? Ben glanced at Graham with curiosity, too.

"Now the questions are, how'd he die and where's his body?" Wyckoff went on. "You both are sure he was dead, right? No possibility that he was still alive? Mind if I have another slice?"

"No way," Ben said. "I mean, yeah, help yourself. But no way he was alive. I checked his pulse myself."

"So much blood." She barely realized she whispered it.

Wyckoff ate his pizza in a few big bites as he watched Graham fidget with his paper plate. "Well, you've got coyotes, vultures, bears. Any of them could have gotten to the remains. The police up there are trying to decide what to do. You realize some charges might come from this?"

She squeezed her eyes shut at the image of vultures fighting over Roland's body.

"Against us?" Ben said. "Are you kidding?"

"I wouldn't worry about it. Without a body, they just have your statements. And if you killed him and moved him, why would you have told them anything at all? It's a pretty easy place to hide a body. I don't think they're in a hurry to arrest anyone with things so sketchy."

Ash pressed her palm over her eyes. Nini, Higman, an unidentified woman. Roland had murdered all these people? And set a house fire? A nightmare had unfolded all around her and she hadn't known anything.

Graham finished folding his plate around his crust and dropped it in the trash. "I guess I'll head out. Thanks for the pizza," he said to Ben. He nodded to Ash. "I'll catch ya' sometime."

She could hardly focus on anything. All she could do was see Roland's calculating gray eyes, in their apartment, the car, the bog. Is that why he took the ring back? To put it on that poor woman's finger? But then she realized Graham had given her an opening.

"Yes," she blurted to his back. "I want to talk to you. Can I text you?"

"Sure. Yeah." He seemed as perplexed as she was.

"All right," she said. "I'll catch up with you later. Cousin."

Graham nodded once, attempting a smile, and walked through the door, bright light silhouetting him.

"I'll go, too." Wyckoff pushed his chair back. "Hold up, Graham, I'll walk with you. You two take care. I'll let you know if I learn anything else."

Wyckoff caught up with Graham on the sidewalk. Graham slouched and looked straight ahead as Wyckoff clapped his hand on his back.

"You're a new man with that haircut, you know? What happened? Did you turn over a new leaf?" When Graham didn't answer, Wyckoff went on. "Did you see that your old boss, Mrs. Borden, was sentenced to twenty-five years? Her turning on you knocked a few years off her sentence, not that she's going to last that long, anyway."

As usual, Graham didn't react and kept walking.

"Hey, we got the results from the autopsy of the body found in your trailer."

"Okay."

"I need to know, Graham, no more being coy." He returned his hand to Graham's shoulder, halting and turning him so they faced each other. It was a rote cop move, designed to both assert power and aggravate. Graham shook off his hand, his eyes narrowed. "What was an old corpse of a junkie doing in your bed?"

Graham took too long to answer. Wyckoff held his breath, trying not to move as Graham appeared to be mulling over something. Was this guy finally about to tell him something, anything, that he could use? All he needed was a tiny opening, a little confession—to any crime—to charge him. And once he charged him, the bargaining could begin. Graham did not want to go to jail. He might provide more information for a better sentence. Wyckoff tried to keep his expression blasé, though he was riveted.

Graham let out a breath. "I don't know, dude. It's as weird to me as it is to you. I'm just glad you figured out who was behind all this so I can rest easy."

Wyckoff sighed. Frustrating. His only success was that he forced Graham to string three complete sentences together. Graham continued toward his car.

"Come on. We both know you're the only person who would have a reason to put it there."

"I don't know that." He kept walking.

"Hey, Graham."

Graham paused, his hand on the driver's door.

"Don't rest too easy."

Chapter 40

GRAHAM pulled away from the curb, giving Cookie a pat. He'd left the car running with the air conditioner streaming, so she was calm and comfortable. God, he'd come too close to telling Wyckoff he'd learned about Roland's plan to kill him and that he planted the corpse. It had almost seemed like a good idea for one moment. Of course, he wouldn't say he found the body while burglarizing Jory's apartment, only that he'd found the dead junky somewhere. Before he said it, he realized moving a corpse was probably a crime. If he'd told Wyckoff even that much, the guy would have booked him. Wyckoff was always watching, eager to pounce. For once, he was almost more alert than Graham.

Graham pulled over and typed in his search bar: "Moving a corpse NYS crime."

"Shit. Felony. Class D." Cookie looked over at the sound of his voice.

That was too close. Christ. Wyckoff had sewn up this case multiple times. This last—and hopefully, final—time, he had even found the true instigator, Roland, skipping nicely over Graham. So why did the guy keep picking at him like some fucking chicken?

It was time to put distance between himself and Wyckoff. He'd find a new place to call home. But where?

Everything had changed. When he'd first learned of his opportunity to inherit millions, he'd been desperate to escape his own assassination. It all unrolled so fast.

Nini, a tiny, crumpled shape down in the cold darkness.

But maybe there was hope. Marco, Ash, Ben. None of them would be here without him.

No. Nothing would offset the pain he'd strewn about like some deranged Johnny Appleseed. All he could do now was keep trying.

And carry the truth to his grave.

Maybe he'd head to Tampa. There was a newly widowed mother there who desperately needed help, even if she didn't realize it yet. He could apply to foster Marco, and they could both go.

His phone beeped a text notice from Ash.

"Hey. Just thinking it might be nice to talk. You want to come to Nini's house for dinner?"

A rush of foreign feelings rattled through him. He was not used to simple kindness. It always seemed to come with a catch. But what catch did Ash possibly present? She wanted nothing from him, except, probably, more information about his side of the family, especially Nini's estranged son, who had fathered Graham. That wasn't bad, though, right? They were cousins. They should learn about each other. But he'd done things. He should say no. Leave and never come back.

Sometimes he didn't listen to his own instincts.

"Can I bring my dog?"

"Of course."

"Okay, yeah. I'll pick up Chinese."

Wyckoff followed Graham to the restaurant, parking across the street. After a few minutes, Graham pushed open the door, carrying two heavy bags. If he saw Wyckoff's car, he ignored it as he set the bags into the back seat.

"Where are you going with so much food?" Wyckoff muttered as he followed Graham out of downtown. Sure enough, he pulled into Nini's driveway, parking behind Ben's hybrid. Wyckoff slowed as he cruised by. This time, Graham looked directly at him as he let the dog out and unloaded the bags.

Wyckoff gave him the cop look, the one that said, "I'm watching you."

As he drove, Wyckoff wondered what he should tell Ash about her cousin. What did she know so far? What, for that matter, did Wyckoff know? His suspicions were strong, his instincts stronger, but his evidence was scant. He doubted Ash would invite her cousin over for dinner if Wyckoff whispered one iota of what he suspected. Where was his responsibility in protecting the innocent? Should she be told what she invited in? And what of the slim chance that Graham had not committed any crimes? Which was worse, staying quiet until he learned more or giving her ample warning?

He wasn't sure if he'd go any further after solving Nini's murder not once, but twice. He knew who pushed her down the stairs: Higman. And he realized who masterminded the plan: Roland. How hard should he work to learn where Graham wedged into the puzzle? Was this man, carrying more food than three people could eat in a week, dangerous to his only living relative?

He must do some soul searching. But for now, he'd let them eat in peace. It was Aiden's bedtime, and Wyckoff needed a hug.

———

Ash called to Graham to come in, and they met in the kitchen. The dog booped Ash's leg with a slow tail wag.

"Hello, pup." She petted the soft back as the dog investigated the kitchen floor.

"I didn't know what you'd like, so I have, uh, sesame chicken, moo shu pork, tofu home style, uh, egg rolls, some veggie dumplings. Let's see, what else?" She'd never seen him nervous, and he pulled the cartons out hastily, setting them on the butcher block for her approval. "Oh, hot and sour soup. Fried noodles."

"Wow, you brought the whole restaurant."

"Hi." Ben said, appearing from the other room. Cookie gave his knee a friendly sniff and settled with a groan on the dining room rug.

"Can I split it with you?" Ash asked.

"What? No. My treat."

"Yeah, but it's a lot. It must have set you back."

Ben smiled, resting one warm hand on Ash's shoulder, the other on Graham's. "You do realize you're the richest people in the county, right? I don't think you need to argue about who pays for the Chinese."

Graham and Ash froze. His surprised expression must have mirrored hers, and they laughed. Bedraggled and exhausted though she was, it was a good laugh. She hadn't done it in far too long, and she suspected Graham hadn't either. Ben joined in.

As it died out, Ash put her hand on Graham's. "We have a lot to get used to, right?"

"Yeah. A lot."

She squeezed his hand then reached for the tofu. "But for now, let's eat. And next time, it's on me."

Author's Note: Thank you for following Ash through this perilous chapter of her journey—I hope it gripped you as much as it did me. But her story doesn't start here. To learn how Ash was thrust into this situation, you'll want to explore the first book in the series, **The River Answered**. *It's the place where betrayals take root, and Ash discovers that the forces behind her Nini's death are greater—and darker—than she imagined. Read on for a peak at The River Answered.*

THE END

About the Author

A.H. Gilbert is an award-winning author known for crafting compelling tales across mystery, horror, disaster, adventure, and short story genres. Her first two novels were honored as finalists for the Killer Nashville Silver Falchion Award, recognizing excellence in mystery and thriller writing. A former newspaper reporter, her investigative work earned a NYS Associated Press award for in-depth reporting.

She lives with her husband on a lush, upstate New York acreage, sharing it with two old mares and a barn cat. Beyond the writing desk, Gilbert channels creative energy into community theater and battles her wild impulses on the golf course. The darker shadows in her imagination roam free within her stories.

First Three Chapters of

The River Answered
By A.H. Gilbert

Chapter 1
The Present

BEFORE she could get home, Nini might be dead.

Ash clutched the steering wheel. The George Washington stretched long over black hell, disappearing in the darkness. Only the trails of taillights showed her it was still there. Time to go.

But her toe refused to press the accelerator.

Cracks splintered Nini's precious, brittle skull. Ash squeezed her eyes to block the image, but it looped through her thoughts. She saw those smart, hazel eyes, edged in dry wrinkles as comfy as fine linen.

Nini always made everything better. Now Ash could help her. She just had to drive northeast over the Catskills to the small hospital in her hometown.

But her foot did not press the pedal.

This damned bridge.

She wiped her damp neck. Even this late, cars dotted the road, streaming around her.

Her heart whirred. Her stomach churned like bubbling lava.

Go. Just go.

She owed her grandmother, Nini, so much, loved her so much. Known to others as Vivian Harrison, Nini helped raise Ash after her mother's death.

Now. Drive.

A glimpse of the dark water. Her hands clenched on the steering wheel, guts lurching.

What if the whole thing crumbles?

Images of cars toppling off the bridge into the water ricocheted across her thoughts.

Blood thumped in her ears. A furious horn blasted from behind. The driver pulled into the next lane, jerking, stopping in time as brakes flashed ahead of him. His passenger window opened as he yelled something at her. His rage drifted around her and away. She sat mute, rabbit still. He continued yelling as his car crawled past hers. He fired his last missive—his middle finger, wagging impotently.

Let's go. Suck it up, squelch the terror. Press the accelerator.

But her foot stayed on the brake.

Something had changed. The worst thing would happen. She knew it. And she knew it wouldn't.

Damn that helpless, drowning dog.

———

A few days before, she and Kaitlyn strode along the river walk in Brooklyn Heights. A cleansing warmth filled her from the early July sun and from her friend's peppy cheerfulness. Was it a glimpse of the world she used to see? At twenty-six, she was stronger than she'd been in a while, her athletic, five-foot-eight frame outpacing her friend.

"I didn't realize I was training for the Olympics here." Kaitlyn's words gasped out between breaths.

Despite the inherent sweatiness of their activity, Kaitlyn had arrived in full make-up. Her olive skin glowed, enhanced with regular trips to a tanning salon. Huge sunglasses perched on her long, slightly crooked nose, hiding her deep-set, dark brown eyes. Her curvy body—so good at giving hugs—was swaddled in a sports bra. One wide strap showed through the neckline of her loose T-shirt. Tight, white leggings clad her generous legs.

"Sorry." Ash's dark brows lifted with her brief smile, arching over her blue-gray eyes. She wore her wavy, light-brown hair in a ponytail. She'd smeared white sunscreen on her straight, narrow nose that rounded at the tip over her plump, pale lips. A few freckles speckled her pale, angular face, her slender neck framed by a purple, V-neck tank top.

Kaitlyn loved to laugh and to see other people happy. A smile from Ash must have been a triumph these days.

Is that a dog?

Something powerful in her psyche roared awake and took control.

The yellow mutt's head was visible above the steely surface of the river. Here at the Upper Bay, the river spread half a mile wide and appeared calm, belying the powerful, tugging currents. The dog seemed to float faster than the water, an odd illusion as it spun in unseen eddies, its front paws splashing weakly.

Save it!

She ran toward the river's edge.

"Hey!"

She didn't hear Kaitlyn's shocked cry or the shrill of the gulls. The birds took off, gleaming white and gray against the deep blue over the Hudson. Manhattan's toothy silhouette hunkered dark in the sun's glare.

The current, lapping against the rocks, seemed to cooperate, swirling the dog toward her. She focused on the desperation in its huge, dark eyes as she prepared to leap.

Her body locked.

An invisible wall shot up from the water's edge.

Not long ago, Ash would have plunged into the river, heedless of her safety, swimming with powerful, steady strokes to the terrified creature. Ash could have navigated the steady current of the Hudson as sure as a dolphin.

But that Ash was gone.

The river rolled at her feet, an icy green menace. Goosebumps tightened on her arms.

The small hand reached through the murky depths, fingers grabbing at nothing. It went limp, waving in the powerful current.

I can't reach it.

The dog sailed by, too far to catch, the river sending it into its churning middle, accelerating. Ash wailed as the little creature became a speck, indistinguishable from other flotsam on the river surface.

She sank into the cool grass, her wail becoming words.

"I couldn't save him. I couldn't save him."

Kaitlyn kneeled beside her. "What's wrong? Stop it!" She gripped Ash's shoulders, giving her rapid, gentle shakes.

A clenching sense of her own uselessness curled Ash on the ground, her back to the river, the scrabbly blades of grass so close they blurred. Blood pulsed through her head, her breathing shallow.

"I hope you weren't planning to jump into that river," Kaitlyn's shock sputtered through her words. "Jesus, you scared me."

Ben's face popped into Ash's thoughts, his brows glowering over the light brown eyes that once smiled at her with humor. She saw the muscles tight in his long jaw, his short, dark hair tousled.

Why now?

Ben, her childhood best friend and former adventure buddy, had nearly become a lover. She barely remembered that delicious warmth glowing from him, extinguished when tragedy tossed them into separate corners of guilt and confusion. After the funeral, she didn't see him again.

She closed her eyes, forcing away the image of his face.

She never cried anymore.

"Ash?"

She sighed, rolled over onto her back, looking at the towering white clouds. One drifted slowly toward the eastern horizon. When she no longer saw it, she looked at Kaitlyn, her scrambled thoughts calming.

"You doing all right?" Kaitlyn sat next to her on the grass, something so uncharacteristic that Ash half-smiled.

"You're going to get your new leggings dirty."

"Yeah, no kidding. I'm probably sitting in dog crap." Kaitlyn glanced around. "I'm going to have to throw these pants in the trash. Serves me right for wearing white. You see how much I love you? I never sit on the ground. That's how much I love you. And now I won't be able to exercise because I'll have no pants."

Ash tried another smile. Kaitlyn's eyes grew round, concern showing through the cushion of humor. Her shoulders dropped a little when Ash smiled.

"You want to go home?" Ash asked.

"Yes. But first, I'd really like to know what the hell just happened."

Ash sighed. "I don't know."

Already, Ash hardly remembered it, and no way could she explain it. A tsunami of terror combined with ... what? Fear? Guilt?

Somewhere in the Hudson, perhaps already in the Sound, a dog struggled, and she had not been able to simply dive in and save it.

"You ready?" Kaitlyn stood and wiped off her leggings, trying to see her backside to evaluate its muddiness.

"Soon." Ash watched the river. She wished she could go back in time.

Chapter 2
July

ASH gasped, yanking the covers off her face.

A boy? No, a dog?

Her pulse swished. Okay, she lay in the warm bed she shared with Roland. Light leaked around the drawn shade. Two p.m. on the phone. That dream left her shaky. What'd happened earlier? It seemed like sketchy lines, half erased. A dog in the Hudson. That was not a dream.

Was it still possible to save it? Animal shelters might know. She unlocked her phone, found a list.

"Animal Shelter," a woman answered.

"Hi, did anyone bring in a dog that was pulled from the river?"

"From what?"

"From the river, just south of Brooklyn Heights. The Upper Bay. I saw a dog, light-colored, long ears. It was going down the river." Her voice sounded strange, reedy. "Black nose. Sweet eyes."

"Today?"

"Yes, this morning."

"Is this your dog?"

"No. I just saw it. In the Hudson. I couldn't reach it."

"Hold on."

She waited, fragmented images of the day and dream flipping in her thoughts. After a few minutes, the woman returned.

"No, ma'am, no dogs came in from the river this morning."

"Oh, okay. I'll try another shelter."

"All right, but ma'am?"

"Yes?"

"I have to tell you, most of them don't make it."

"What?"

"If they're in the river. Most of them drown before anyone can get to them. They find drowned dogs down the south end of the harbor all the time."

Ash sucked in her breath and held it. She failed to click the "end" button fast enough to beat the images in her mind.

She tried the next number.

The bedroom door opened in a flood of light as Roland's face appeared. Her stomach clenched. He shouldn't know.

"Who are you talking to?"

"I'm trying to find out if someone pulled that dog out of the river."

He sat next to her, putting his arm around her.

"Don't." He tried gently to take her phone. She pulled away as someone answered.

"Hello. I'm wondering. Did someone bring in a dog today that was rescued from the river?"

"The river? Nope. None from the river today. I've been here all day."

"Okay, thank you." She hung up and dialed the next shelter.

"Stop." This time, he pulled the phone from her hands.

Her tears mechanism seemed broken.

"But I need to know if he got out."

"I'm sure it did. But the shelters probably won't be able to tell you. Probably someone pulled it out and kept it, or it had the owner's information on the collar, and he's back home, safe and sound."

She got up and opened the blinds, the sunlight hurting. It hadn't worn a collar.

Traffic floated along the busy street. Two kids ran down the sidewalk past a couple with a stroller and a schnauzer straining on its leash. Ash looked for her jeans. She spotted them on their soft, blue chair, under Roland's latest book, *The Devil's Chessboard* by David Talbot.

194

Distracted, she picked it up along with her jeans and looked at its red cover.

"Conspiracies?"

"CIA." He moved close to her "What are you doing?"

"You like that spy stuff, don't you?"

He took it and placed it on the bedside table. "No, I mean, why are you getting your jeans?"

She pulled them on, catching her new engagement ring on the denim. She wasn't used to wearing rings, especially not one with a high profile. "I'm going to walk along the bank to see if I can find it."

"No! You shouldn't go back out there." Roland's glassy-gray eyes looked almost clear in the bright light. Her fiancé's mysterious eyes, wide behind his small, round glasses, still mesmerized her. A striking contrast to his short-cropped, auburn hair and dark brows, his clear gray eyes seemed to see the future. He moved to her, two inches taller, and a bit soft in the middle, with wide shoulders so good at engulfing her in hugs.

"But I really need to know if it's okay."

"Listen to me. You saw that dog in the river two days ago. You're not going to find it out there today."

"Two days?" She pulled back and unlocked her phone. She saw multiple missed calls from Kaitlyn. How had she lost so much time?

"You need to take a step back from this, babe." His voice was soft. "Your reaction to that dog is …."

She turned away. Her thoughts grew muddy. He paused and tried again.

"I'm just worried about you. It almost sounds like, I mean, Ash. It just seems, and I say this with all the love you know I have in my heart for you, but it's maybe a bit…irrational. No, no! I mean, unrealistic. Don't take this the wrong way, but I get the feeling … did something happen to

195

you? I mean, in the past, with water … an accident? Maybe on the Yough?"

He pronounced it "Yock," like "rock," as she'd taught him, as she'd taught hundreds of tourists before paddling toward the rapids. All those tourists, all the rapids on the Youghiogheny. They launched on the calm spot near Friendsville in Maryland and hauled out some five miles later after navigating almost continuous rapids.

"It's pronounced 'Yock-uh-gay-nee,'" she'd tell them. "Learn how to say it, because you're going to want to tell your friends about this."

She guided hundreds of tourists with no major accidents.

Except one.

On her last run.

Now she stared at Roland. Words seemed impossible.

She'd told him she'd been a white-water guide but not much else. A real conversation would force her to think about that day. She remembered little. Her mind had closed it away, that last run down the Yough, three years ago. It fed her bits in dreaded flashes or nightmares. She couldn't describe what happened that terrible August day.

One thing she knew: She did not want to talk about it. She couldn't even admit it ever happened, especially not to her fiancé. She refused to jeopardize his safe, solid love.

"The Yough? Why would you ask that?" Her words blurted, rushed and stumbling like a guilty drunk. "Nothing happened on the Yough, not that's worth talking about."

Worth? No. How dare she assign a value to what she did? Ash pressed both palms against her face, forcing her thoughts away from the conversation, looking around for something else to focus on. Damn this fogginess.

He put his hand over hers. "Well, I don't know, but I made some calls while you were sleeping."

"Calls?"

"Yes. To a couple doctors. I found one who can talk to you today."

"Doctors? What? I'm okay. What do you mean?" Why did he always want to fix her?

"Well, I mean psychiatrists." He paused for a breath, watching her before adding, "I called a few while you were resting. One can see you at 5:45."

No!

There was nothing wrong with her. That's what she wanted to say. Her thoughts jumped around. The events at the river with Kaitlyn seemed vague and distant. That dog, the lost time. Roland's concern, in the opposite of what he intended, she knew, made it worse.

She should comfort him, so he'd stop acting like she was nuts. Why that dog, now of all times? Roland had proposed three nights ago, and now her nutty behavior scared him. They should be happy, excited, considering all kinds of delightful details about the event that would formally join them, setting them on a new journey together. What if she scared him away?

Her body hummed with the urge to fall back asleep. A quiet part of her didn't care about anything. She sank back in the bed.

"Will you go see her?"

It wouldn't help, but she didn't dare say that to him. "Yes, all right."

"Oh, good. I'll call her to confirm."

"Okay, thanks. I'm just going to stay in here for a little while."

"Okay. Do you want me to come back and lie with you?"

"No, it's okay."

He brushed back her hair and kissed her forehead, more like a father than a fiancé. "I'm worried about you." He shut the door behind him with a quiet click, like a nurse leaving a drowsy patient.

She grabbed her phone.

"Westside SPCA."

"Hi, I need to know if someone brought you a dog today, or maybe, a couple days ago, one that they got out of the river?"

"Miss, you already called us."

"Okay, but it might have come in since then."

"It didn't. You need to stop calling."

This stranger was right, and so was Roland.

Just stop.

Too much tangled up inside her.

"Okay. But can you promise me one thing?"

"What?"

"If it comes in, will you call me?"

The woman sighed. Ash imagined her standing in a tiny, dismal office, wearing a tee shirt dotted with dirt and saliva, annoyed, tired of caring. The building likely smelled of feces and bleach and the woman's head and soul must ache from the constant clamor in the kennels.

The dogs barked. "Help! Help!"

"Yes, okay, I promise. I'll put your number by the phone."

"Oh, thank you! And my name. It's Ash Harrison. You have the number, right?"

The woman read it to her and repeated her name.

"That's right. Thank you so much."

That promise calmed her.

Would the psychiatrist understand this dog was the problem, or would she try to root through Ash's brain as if digging for an olive in a jar?

It would be a farce. She'd go to appease Roland, but she would not try to explain herself. Plus, it would be expensive, and she had no job. Roland said he made enough. She didn't want to share these simmering thoughts—that dog, her escalating fears, these changes for the worse— she would not let it all be scrutinized, prodded, dissected.

198

Her thoughts were hard, but they didn't hurt.

But what she refused to think about burned a hole straight through her soul.

Chapter 3
June, The Previous Month

GRAHAM had already lost one dangerous game. He damn well wouldn't lose another.

He couldn't go straight until he paid for his freedom. Right. As a hardware store clerk, paying back $300,000 to a cartel kingpin was impossible. Shit, his salary barely covered food and Cookie's annual vet bill.

He needed the money fast. Raising that kind of coin, while preventing his own torture, murder or enslavement, meant he had to be creative. The law was secondary.

For the moment. Not forever.

A bird's clear trill breezed through the brush. Towhee or a cardinal? His father had taught him a couple of calls. A fucking puzzle, that one. A dangerous, drunken felon who was most comfortable in the woods. Dear Dad liked to identify the birds before using them for target practice.

Graham squatted, leaning against the tree and pulling a pack of cigarettes from the gray, flannel shirt he wore unbuttoned over a black tee. The dry smoke numbed his raw lungs. This steep hike always brought up globs of brown gunk. Cookie stepped around the back of the tree, poking him with her nose before moseying off. He trailed his hand along her chunky, wet back. The rain-spattered undergrowth made her stinky, and she left a smear of white hairs on his jeans.

So, now he rented out a cabin he didn't own to meth cookers. Chump change. To make enough, he agreed to sell them their key ingredient, ephedrine, stolen from a nearby pharmaceutical plant. The employee who stole it was in trouble, but he couldn't identify the guy he sold it to. Graham had worn a mask.

It was damn good stuff, and it would cook up nice. That's where the money was.

But if Luis found out, Graham would be the one cooked.

Even at five-foot, ten inches, Graham seemed small. His narrow hips meant his pants slipped despite the wide, black leather belt. His slight shoulders and chest were knotted tight with practical muscle built by lifting things like tires and car batteries. The callouses on his hands came from reaming on frozen bolts, drawing a bowstring and scaling trees. His flat, greenish-blue eyes, partially obscured by light brown bangs, betrayed nothing.

He'd climbed the hill to check the tiny cabin one last time before those guys moved their crap in. Porcupines' gnawing had left odd holes in the door and windowsills. Inside, under its sticky dust, it housed two, ancient, handmade, wooden chairs and a matching table, their once-white paint yellowed and chipped. Rodents had chewed the canvas on the army cot.

Nothing a broom and some mousetraps wouldn't fix. Get the hand pump going. It would work for two, pointy-headed Pittsburgh street dealers who'd found their way to sleepy Mill Valley, answering a perverted proprietorial call to cook meth. The biggest problem with them is they would stand out. Jory wore a high, blond-tipped afro and a red neck tattoo. Flower shaved his head and stuck a steel toothpick through his eyebrow. Graham needed to introduce them to work boots and John Deere ball caps.

During his father's few lucid periods, he brought Graham to these woods he knew as a child. Didn't matter that some old bat down the gravel road owned them. His father acted like he owned the place and that rubbed off on Graham. Renting out the remote cabin seemed like a natural outgrowth.

He stood, stretched and walked around back where a ramshackle woodshed leaned against the cabin's outside wall. The woodshed door was easy to miss, a crooked, hinged board over a narrow slot, wide enough for a thin man but not a thick one. He pulled down a wad of burlap from the rafters. What looked like insulation hid a twelve-gauge shotgun and a box of shells. Graham cracked it open. Still sleek and smooth. The shells, all slugs, were dry, boxed and protected by a plastic bag. He put both the gun and the shells back, hidden from view. Just in case, his father said. In case of what? He couldn't ask his father. Died in prison when Graham was twelve.

It didn't matter why. Hiding a gun, just in case, had become a family tradition, apparently. Graham liked it there, and Jory and Flower would never find it. They weren't explorers, only stupid meth cookers.

Graham, always teetering on the edge of survival, like the solid security of that shotgun. His father delivered nothing he could count on, appearing without warning and disappearing for months or years. He seemed to want to be important to Graham and his mother, but his cruelty, his drunken mania, made him terrifying, offering nothing of value, certainly not money. But when his mother got her hands on some cash, she put it up her nose or in her arm. Starting young, Graham focused on finding food, staying warm, and getting in the first punch.

When he hit fifteen, Luis' guys had him selling meth. Then he moved into Luis' downtown headquarters, a narrow four-story brick building on State Street. His belly full of real food for the first time in his life,

Graham thought he finally had someone he could count on. Selling didn't even seem risky with Luis around.

Later, he realized Luis was the risk. You don't mess with the Cartel. Graham teetered in a dangerous place. Any delusions about that got crushed the night he saw what Luis' guys did to one of his dealers who tried to quit. Until then, Graham hadn't realized how loudly a tibia could snap.

They dragged that guy out and nobody ever saw him again.

Everything Graham knew ended when the cops snagged him during a $250,000 transaction. He, his youth and his fool-ass dreams were sentenced to five years of hard time in the Auburn Correctional Facility. It should have been fifteen, but Luis' excellent lawyer argued it down. It wasn't out of kindness. The more favors Graham owed him, the better for Luis. Luis hadn't bothered to visit, but he sent a message through another inmate. "Keep your mouth shut and figure out how you'll pay it back."

That debt hung over him every second in jail, and it'd been his constant companion in the two years since his release.

God, it took a year before he got the prison stench off his skin. That sick stink of sweat, metal and Lysol. Even though he scrubbed himself, he could smell it every day. It'd followed him out.

But his youth and those dreams, they never made it out.

Now, he lit a fuse that could lead straight to the dynamite. If Luis learned someone was cooking in volume here, he'd want to know who. And if he even got a whiff of Graham, well, Graham better be ready to pay back the $300,000. The only other choices included servitude in perpetuity to Luis or a slow, tortuous death. He preferred to pay. But he had to be careful. He couldn't be discovered until he got all the money. Luis wouldn't accept partial payments.

After this, he'd go straight. For real.

❧❧

You've just read the first three chapters of the
first, exciting, Ash Harrison mystery,
The River Answered.

Want more?
Check out this and all **A.H. Gilbert's** books on Amazon.

www.ingramcontent.com/pod-product-compliance
Lightning Source LLC
Chambersburg PA
CBHW060926120626
46557CB00003B/894